"Most of you reading this will be using a space-made product in your lifetime; some of you will be making these products in space; and a few of you will be very rich because you bet on the right horse, risked your life savings, and worked like hell to make it happen."

G. Harry Stine

"I think I can honestly say that Stine is one of the most provocative and imaginative thinkers in the area today. I am delighted that readers now have the opportunity to explore his views of our future that so many of us in science, engineering, and the arts have enjoyed for so long in private conversation with him."

Gene Rodenberry, Producer of *Star Trek*

". . . .not one but *all* of our crisis problems can be solved by exploiting space. Employment, inflation, pollution, population, energy, running out of nonrenewable resources—there is a pie in the sky for the U.S.A. and for the entire planet including the impoverished 'Third World.' I won't try to prove it here. See *The Third Industrial Revolution* by G. Harry Stine."

Robert A. Heinlein

The Space Enterprise

G. HARRY STINE

Illustrations by Rick Sternbach

SF
ACE BOOKS
A Division of Charter Communications Inc.
A GROSSET & DUNLAP COMPANY
51 Madison Avenue
New York, New York 10010

THE SPACE ENTERPRISE
Copyright © 1980 by G. Harry Stine
Illustrations copyright © 1980 by Rick Sternbach

An ACE Book

First Ace printing: August 1980

First Mass Market Printing: January 1982

Published simultaneously in Canada

2 4 6 8 0 9 7 5 3 1

Manufactured in the United States of America

ACKNOWLEDGMENTS

Although some of the ideas, concepts, and analyses in this book are my own, I certainly cannot lay claim to all of them. I have acted as a synthesist, drawing from the work of many people, basing what is written here on long conversations, correspondence, and reading. The ethic of science and technology not only requests that I recognize them, but my own personal appreciation for them will not permit me to do otherwise. Without them and others whom I may have inadvertantly neglected to mention, the space enterprise would remain only an idea in the lonely mind of someone — for no one person is the originator of the concept. They deserve at least this mention of their contribution, large or small, to the space enterprise, because the future will want to know who brought it about: Dr. Isaac Asimov, James Patrick Baen, Christian O. Basler, Dr. Ivan Bekey, Ben Bova, Dr. Alan W. Burg, Dan Cassidy, Arthur C. Clarke, Richard A. Colla, J. Frank Coneybear, Dr. Carleton S. Coon, Gerald W. Driggers, Bruce W. Dunbar, Frederick C. Durant III, Dr. Krafft A. Ehricke, Dr. Sven W. Englund, Mark Frazier, Don Fuqua, Dr. Peter E. Glaser, Barry M. Goldwater, Charles L. Gould, Philomena G. Grodzka, Paul S. Hans, Robert A. Heinlein, H. Keith Henson, Alan B. Hazard, Barbara Marx Hubbard, Gary Hudson, Maxwell W. Hunter, A. D. Kasanowski, Dr. Walter Morgan, Dr. Gerard K. O'Neill, Dr. Robert W. Prehoda, Dr. John R. Pierce, Dr. Jerry Pournelle, Jesco von Puttkammer, Ralph A. Rockow, Gene Roddenberry, Robert Salkeld, Dr. Harrison H. Schmitt, Dr. Charles Sheffield, Paul L. Siegler, Dr. Ralph Sklarew, Richard D. Stutzke, Olin Teague, Georg von Tiesenhausen, Alvin Toffler, and Dr. J. Peter Vajk. Please also add to this list those who are no long able to take part in the space enterprise: Dr. Wernher von Braun, John Woods Campbell, Jr., Dandridge M. Cole, and Dr. Willy Ley. Coming from all fields of human endeavor, all of them and more are the reason why the space enterprise is happening now.

G. Harry Stine
Phoenix, Arizona
June 15, 1979

"Men, my brothers, men the workers, ever
    reaping something new:
That which they have done but earnest of the
    things that they shall do:
For I dipt into the future, far as human eye
    could see,
Saw the Vision of the world, and all the
    wonder that would be;
Saw the heavens fill with commerce, argo-
    sies of magic sails,
Pilots of the purple twilight, dropping down
    with costly bales; . . .
Not in vain the distance beacons. Forward,
    forward let us range.
Let the great world spin for ever down the
    ringing grooves of change.
Thro' the shadow of the globe we swept
    into the younger day:
Better fifty years of Europe than a cycle of
    Cathay.
Mother Age (for mine I knew not) help me as
    when life begun;

Rift the hills, and roll the waters, flash the
    lightnings, weigh the Sun—
O, I see the crescent promise of my spirit
    hath not set.
Ancient fountains of inspiration well thro'
    all my fancy yet . . ."

"Locksley Hall," Alfred, Lord Tennyson,
1809–1892

This book is respectfully dedicated to:

Those who gave us the technology, the capital, the social systems, and the philosophies that are the foundations of the space enterprise.

Those who are now working to make the space enterprise the reality of today and the hope of the future.

And those who, in the future, will bring the space enterprise to fruition.

The Space Enterprise

Prologue

As this is written in 2050 *Anno Domini*, with the Twenty-First Century as its mid-point and all around us the human race blossoming into maturity, the words of Tennyson now 200 years old take on new meaning. A century ago, these words were only partially quoted, and the prophecy of the "heavens filled with commerce" was interpreted to apply to aviation, the transportation of goods and services through the thin envelope of the Earth's atmosphere. Today we know that Tennyson may have been seeing much further than that limited view of a century ago. He may have unconsciously forecast a human activity in the heavens which far transcended anything that aviation accomplished and that had shaped the beginning of the third millenium far differently than the pessimists of our recent adolescence could possibly have imagined in their wildest and most controversial forecasts. Even the optimistic forecasters such as Herman Kahn, Dr. Krafft Ehricke, and Barbara Marx Hubbard could not fully grasp the implications, although they tried.

The single factor that changed the course of the history of mankind was the slow realization that we were not trapped forever on the treadmill cage of our home planet, Earth; that we were a universal species capable of expanding into the Universe, and of using the Universe; that we were emerging from the womb of Mother Earth into the open system of the Universe.

The pioneers sensed it. They began by calling it "space flight." Then it took on the more respectable and professional label of "astronautics" (star sailing) and "cosmonautics" (Universe sailing). From "space exploration" and Armstrong's "giant leap for mankind" (whose meaning was not understood for years) it became "space industrialization," "space utilization," "space exploitation," "The Third Industrial Revolution," and "The Space Enterprise."

Without it and without the economic motives and desire to improve one's lot by profitable activities in space—in short, without the incentive to "make a buck"—the Twenty-First Century might have been the beginning of the New Dark Ages, the final gasp of humanity against the limits to further growth on a finite planet. Instead, it opened the doors to our adulthood as a species.

No longer do the steel mills, smelters, and forges belch their smoke, ashes, and particulates into our planetary atmosphere.

No longer do petroleum refineries choke our air with sulphurous emissions and glaring flames of flare gas.

No longer do nuclear power plants dot the landscape, their fail-safe circuits poised to prevent any possible accident that might release radioactivity.

No longer do the coal trains wind their snakelike ways over the railroads from the strip mines that destroyed local ecologies to the coal-fired electrical plants that provided needed electricity but also dumped copious amounts of radioactive carbon-14 into the atmosphere from burning the coal.

No longer do we burn precious coal and petroleum, but instead convert them into recyclable chemical feedstocks.

No longer are people chained to the dreary repetition of the production lines reminiscent of the First

Industrial Revolution, spending hour after hour doing exactly the same operation on identical products moving past, always at the urging to work faster.

No longer are people alone, for they can be in instant communication with anyone at any time and from any location on Earth or in space; nor do they need to become lost because modern electronics and satellites can locate them in an instant and tell others where they are.

No longer do the electric lights glow dimly brown or go out for lack of energy, for it comes to us in abundance from geosynchronous orbit on a power beam . . . or from solar power screens to run the photoelectrolysis hydrogen generator on a rooftop, providing individual installations with decentralized power.

No longer does half the human race languish in illiteracy for there are television screens in the most remote countries, powered by solar energy and able to receive a wide variety of educational and entertainment programs directly from space.

And no longer does anyone go hungry. Weather satellites now permit us to make reliable weather *predictions* for an entire growing season while other satellites watch the Sun for indications of changes or emissions that would affect the Earth's upper atmosphere and thus cause weather changes by processes now well-understood. Earth resources satellites now keep track of crop growth and hazards, productivity, and the success of new food grain hybrids developed with the bio-technology from orbiting laboratories.

Even in the low-tech nations of the globe, the space enterprise has made the difference between barbarism, famine, disease, and poverty—and a relative well-being that could not have been imagined a hundred years ago. They now have abundant energy from space and the availability of both products and services from beyond the atmosphere . . . for it is as easy to program a load of steel to land at Acra as at Akron.

It took the systems engineering approach that was developed for the immense and complex tasks of the space enterprise in order to begin applying the benefits of space to the low-tech cultures of Earth. The products and services that were needed by the high-tech countries were not necessarily those that were needed or useful to the low-tech countries. Systems engineering revealed an exceedingly high degree of human compassion in solving the problems of adapting the space enterprise to low-tech nations and their problems.

$E = mc^2$. This basic equation of the Universe from the Twentieth Century no longer has the ambivalent connection with nuclear energy and nuclear weapons. It now means that wherever human beings have energy and mass to work with, they can live and prosper. And they have done this not only on Earth because of the growing activities in space, but they have also done it in space throughout the Solar System. The results of the 2050 census will probably show that, for the first time, there are over a million people living in space. We are almost *everywhere* in the Solar System . . . or soon will be. There are people on Mercury, in orbit around Venus, on and in the Moon, on Mars, in the planetoid belt by the thousands, on the valuable Gallilean satellites of Jupiter and even in Jupiter's upper atmosphere, the chemical golconda of the Solar System. We're looking at the satellites of Saturn now. The latest rumors speak of a claim-staking expedition to both Uranus and Neptune. Pluto will feel that "one small step" before too many years have passed.

The human race would now survive a nuclear catastrophe. We have gotten all our eggs out of a single planetary basket. Soon, we will be on our way to the stars; when that happens, the sun can die and the human race that sprang from its hellfires will live on in the Universe.

We are engaged in two major enterprises: the habitation of the Solar System (which is a prelude to the stars) and the terraforming of planets. Our first attempt at terraforming—making a planet into a comfortable Earth-like home for people—is Planet Earth. It will take a few more centuries, but we should be able, now that we have stabilized population, to return it more or less to the condition it was in 50,000 years ago when our ancestors evolved upon it in an environment we still find most comfortable physically and psychologically.

There are still wars . . . and there will probably always be wars and other physical conflicts because we are a violent species. This characteristic may save us at some unknown time in the future if and when we meet up with another violent species among the stars. But, when we do meet them, we will at least do so with the new ethic of metalaw guiding our actions, with Haley's Rule to advise us to "do unto others as they would have you do unto them." We will go to the stars prepared ethically and morally with a mature philosophy to guide our actions. And we will be prepared to fight to survive if necessary.

We have yet to see an interplanetary war. Such a thing may be impossible. The balance of terror of the thermonuclear age has unfortunately followed us into Earth-Moon space, in spite of the fact that many of us believe that nationalism should stop at the stratosphere. But it didn't. Rather than ignore it, we have learned to live with and to control it as best we can. The Attilas of the world still roam, and they roam in space as well. But they may not be able to roam beyond our twin planet system of Earth-Moon. The Solar System is rapidly filling up with people who have had their bellies full of the threat of war. The planetoids are about as independent as any culture we have yet seen, and the area is full of social experiment groups who do not want their important social laboratory conditions contaminated by outsiders. Yes, we may have to throw a few rocks at Earth at some point, because the seats of power are still there and the distrust of remote management still grows in spite of modern instant communications. Nobody wants to, and we may make it through this difficult transition as we made it through the thermonuclear period with everyone afraid to be the first and afraid of the consequences. We got through October 1961; we'll manage to make it through similar crises. I've become an optimist.

But the stars still beckon, and we may be able to make it after all in spite of having to remain well below light-speed. It really doesn't make any difference if it takes a century to make the trip now because a single crew can do the job. Out of the space laboratories in weightlessness came a whole new approach to longevity in addition to the biotechnologies that completely conquered all disease (including the common cold, but there are few people who remember what that ailment was), perfected cloning techniques that allow modern bio-technicians to install replacement organs cloned from your own tissue (I'm on my second cloned kidney and my first cloned aortal arch), and finally mapped the human genetic code to permit couples to select the best children they can jointly conceive.

How primitive medical technology of a century ago seems to us today! Why, dentistry was so brutal that they had to drill the decay out of dental caries and plug the holes with *metal*. There was no caries immunization—nor dental regeneration. Without the biotechnology labs in space, making use of weightlessness, high vacuum, and broad temperature extremes, none of this would have been possible this soon; we might still be waiting for some bureaucrat to give a health safety clearance to permit it to be done in an earthbound laboratory.

In spite of the million people out here in the Solar System already, this is still a frontier, and a deadly one at that. It kills the stupid people quickly. Only the bright ones survive, those who are willing to listen to the instruction and advice of the old timers and follow it. It's fairly comfortable now at Luna City and at L-5; the reports from Kosmoyarsk at L-4 indicate that it may be a little more spartan there, but that doesn't bother the Soviets, it seems; they are used to that sort of life-style and have been for over a century. But the camps and outposts around Mars, Jupiter, and in the planetoid belt can be pretty grim and bare; you still have to wear a pressure suit to get around between modules. There's greenery at L-5 now, and the hydroponic gardens in the Moon have finally eliminated the need for the Loonies to get their water and oxygen from lunar rocks.

Unfortunately, there are some ghost towns already. The people miscalculated in some cases. Solar flares came along and blew out their candles because they didn't have a storm cellar or enough shielding. Or they didn't get the patch slapped on the meteorite puncture fast enough. Or a whole list of things. Old John W. Campbell was right; pioneering amounts to discovering new and more horrible ways to die.

One group—I don't know how they talked a shuttle captain into lifting them off Earth in the first place—went out to the Second Lagrangian Point, probably the most unstable of the Lagrangian Points, which is why there wasn't anybody there. This outfit wanted to prove to the world that they didn't need high technology. They were going to survive by "mind over matter," sort of a religion with them. Obviously, they didn't survive very long at all after the shuttle skipper left them where they wanted to be according to contract terms. The Guard had to do a mop-up operation in conjunction with the Soviet L-4 detachment because the debris was right in the Earth-Moon shipping lanes after it spread out a little bit.

The transfer of heavy industry off Earth caused some early problems of course, because of the need to re-train a lot of people, some of whom didn't want to be re-trained. But when they found the new assembly industries, craftsmanship industries, and services industries that came about to take advantage of the new materials that came from space factories—some that had never existed before—there was a slow but orderly transition. The building and construction boom on Earth absorbed a lot of the mechanics and craftsmen; as new materials became available from space, some of them revolutionized construction techniques on Earth. New construction was required, anyway, to up-date homes and buildings to use the new energy technologies of the hydrogen economy and the solar power gadgetry . . . to say nothing of building new ones designed around these technologies in the first place. The Twenty-First Century home is as different from a Twentieth Century house as that house is from a cave. (To some extent, however, the resemblance to a cave is still there because, in spite of technology, people still want a better-upholstered cave to live in.)

There also had to be a major change in work habits on Earth. In spite of strong religious and ideological reactions, the Protestant "work ethic" slowly evolved into what some people term the "quaternary economic systems technology" (QUEST) ethic. This derives from Herman Kahn's division of economic activity, the quarternary being that work which is done for its own sake, such as research, entertainment, the creative arts, exploration, etc. With the improved educational systems made possible by the communications/information revolution caused by comsats, the general educational level of the population of the world was raised; in the high-tech nations most affected by space industrialization, this eventually led to the QUEST ethic where people did the sort of work they liked to do, were able to get the training and education through the satellite TV links, and were able to find the markets through these same links. We tend to forget how poorly educated most people were before the comm/info revolution that peaked about 2001.

We also tend to take for granted the tremendous variety of creative work that now surrounds us in literature, in the graphic arts, and in the performing arts. The comm/info revolution spearheaded this, of course, but without the expanding frontier of space to stimulate new and fresh outlooks, the creative revolution would have been stillborn or, worse yet, antagonistic to the technology that made it possible, a situation similar to the early 1900 artists of all sorts who developed an anti-technology approach; no wonder they couldn't understand what was happening to the world!

Early science-fiction—Heinlein, the Robinsons—touched briefly upon the impact of the high frontier upon the creative arts. Indeed, we do have weightless ballet today along with its offshoot, zero-g gymnastics. But Arthur C. Clarke was one of the few who forecast the explosion in the creative arts that accompanied the thrust into space. Early space graphic artists—Bonestell, McCall, Sternbach, Davis, Freas, and others—merely scratched the surface of the subject matter . . . until they got out there and were able to draw it from real life. Sunrise on the Moon occurs so slowly that you can paint it in real time. Space was far more pictorial and far more interesting than anyone had expected. In fact, it gave us new perspectives with which to look at the creative arts of Earth. Stereosculpture with holograms, video illustration, and electronic graphics took their place alongside the synthesizer music of 1970 as art forms making full use of technology. The art forms developing around the technology of neuroelectronics are something else again and are already opening up whole new vistas for artists who are directly inputting the human nervous system of their customers with a full range of sensory data, all created electronically.

Once unleashed, the creative energies of human beings will always make full and complete use of the technology available. This has been true from the earliest cave paintings to the present neuroelectronic arts.

How narrow, primitive, and restricted our world view of both art and science was a mere century ago!

In fact, looking back to 1980, I wonder at how very primitive we really were in almost every area!

But we made it after all.

It started with only a few people who simultaneously grasped, each in their different ways because of their individual backgrounds, the magnitude of the great change that could occur, the all-emcompassing nature of this space enterprise, and the fact that it led to a hopeful future. Believe me, those early years of the concept were not easy ones. There were times when the whole affair threatened to go down the tubes. When the Space Shuttle *Columbia* was over a year late in flying its first orbital mission, many of us thought that the game was up, that we had lost. Then, when they bent the re-built *Enterprise* and lost the whole crew, we were afraid that the public outcry would cause the whole thing to collapse . . . but it didn't. And the small group of advocates hung on, believing that their dream was rational and therefore inevitable . . . and it was. As the years went by, more and more people joined the club, realizing that although the space enterprise would not solve all of the problems of the future, it was at least the key to opening up the system so that the problems became *solvable*. The Soviets brought the first products back from space, but it was, in the final analysis, the Americans who made the whole thing pay off in spite of bureaucracy, red tape, government and corporate lethargy, and a surprising lack of nerve on the part of a lot of astronautics experts. It was the Americans, racing like hell with the Japanese and West Germans, who vindicated such early entrepeneurs as Basler, Henson, Sheffield, and Frazier. And, even at that, it wouldn't have been done without the political support from Teague, Schmitt, Stevenson, and Fugua, who were among the first to get bills rammed through Congress to provide incentives for the space entrepreneurs. The incredible wealth generated for America and its government by these measures has repaid the initial investments a thousandfold.

How strange it seems to have witnessed *all* of it! How little did we realize that the synergy of technology would advance geriatrics and longevity so that we could! And it's only been 70 years, at that! The Prehoda Institute tells me every time I go back for a check-up that I've got another 50 years . . . and they keep updating that all the time. It is even strange to think back and realize that the original edition whose text is here was originally published on *paper*, that *trees* were cut down in order to permit its printing so that other people could read it. How far we have come in publishing so that now, with a thin plastic diskkette covered with iron oxide, you can input this to your electronic book and read it while those trees that would have provided paper still stand.

I can't see those trees from here. Perhaps soon we will have some growing here anyway, but it's nice to go back every once in a while, just to smell the earth and see the sky and feel the breeze at your back. Even without those things, living here in space is much better. It's as though we were really meant to be here all along. Perhaps we were. But it took a lot of work to do it.

We *could* do it.

We *had* to do it.

And we *did* do it.

And all of us have a future to look forward to as a result.

—G. Harry Stine
La Grange Five Space Settlement
26 March, 2050

CHAPTER ONE

On July 10, 1962, a milestone in human progress was passed with little or no public notice. Yet this occurrence was to have the most profound effect upon people all over the world, and the consequence would far exceed the most sanguine expectations of nearly everyone except a few far-thinking individuals who had seen it coming and who could glimpse the possible results. It was the opening of a whole new realm of human activity in a totally new frontier. It had never happened before in all recorded history. And it carried with it the promise of better lives for everyone, and their children and their children's children . . . provided they used it wisely.

On that date, a small, 77-kilogram (170 pound) satellite called *Telstar* was launched into orbit around the Earth. It wasn't the first satellite; that honor belongs solely and forevermore to the Soviet *Sputnik-I* launched on October 4, 1957. But it was the world's first commercial satellite, the first attempt to *use* space to solve problems on Earth, the first satellite to be bought, paid for, built, and operated by private enterprise rather than a government agency. *Telestar* was a communications relay satellite making use of the "high ground" or exceptional vantage point of

Earth orbital space to receive radio signals, travelling in a straight line, from Earth below, and to transmit them back to another point on the spherical Earth far beyond the line-of-sight of the original transmitting station.

Telstar opened the space frontier for *use* by people rather than for the exploration by a selected few. But it was alone; people were yet to follow it.

Another milestone was passed on September 17, 1976 during the 200th year of the United States of America, a country built upon the foundations of individual freedom, responsibility, and opportunity to better oneself by taking great risks, working hard, and providing something of value to one's fellow human. In the cool, bright morning of the Mohave Desert at Palmdale, California, a totally new type of human transportation vehicle rolled into the sunlight for the first time. It was the Space Shuttle Orbiter *Enterprise*, the sixth vehicle in the history of the United States to carry that illustrious and appropriate name . . . and the first of a new breed of spaceships. The *Enterprise* was the first of the Space Shuttles, designed and built for the specific purpose of permitting people to travel into Earth orbit and back on an everyday basis and thus putting the space frontier at the doorstep of everyone.

These two milestones are significant because they mark, respectively, the beginning of the unmanned and manned *utilization* of the Solar System.

Telstar was a milestone because it put to use for the first time the orbital space around the Earth for commercial purposes. It was owned by a government-regulated private enterprise, American Telephone and Telegraph Company; unlike a government operation, any person in the world could have stepped up on July

10, 1962 and purchased part of AT&T in the form of capital stock; that person could then have participated in any of the profit that would accrue to AT&T because of the commercial utilization of space with *Telstar*. The first commercial communications satellite actually didn't make any money; it wasn't really intended to because it was a "pilot project," leading the way for its progeny, the communications satellites that would and did make money because of the service they provided and still provide today.

The Space Shuttle Orbiter *Enterprise* and its sister ships *Columbia, Challenger, Discovery,* and *Atlantis* are milestones because they permit people to go into space on a regular basis to use the space environment. All previous space vehicles have been used once and only once, then splashed into the ocean or retired as museum pieces once their single missions were completed. The *Mercurys, Geminis,* and *Apollos* (we don't know whether or not the Soviets re-use all or part of their *Soyuz* spacecraft) were exploration ships. In common with other exploration ships that have traveled Earth's seas and skies, they were highly specialized vehicles, built at great cost and with the very best available technology, designed to perform a single function, and thereafter useless for exploiting what they had explored. The Space Shuttles will fly again and again, like commercial airliners. Although the Shuttles will be piloted by highly trained people, ordinary people will be able to ride along into space without undue discomfort after passing a simple physical exam and taking a few months to learn how to live and work in space. Space Shuttle payload space is for sale—expensive, but for sale. Payloads need only conform to safety requirements established to protect the Shuttle and its crew.

The space of the Solar System has already been used to provide services for profit and a return on investment. The space of the Solar System is now opening up, as this is being written, for people to go out there and *do things*.

Thus, in the decade since Neil A. Armstrong set foot on the Moon, making that "small step for a man," we have learned what he meant by that "giant leap for mankind." Our entire thinking about space has undergone radical and drastic change.

To many people, this whole matter of space, a space program, or future activities in space is anathema. On the other hand, many Americans are very proud of our achievements in space exploration. The National Air and Space Museum of the Smithsonian Institution in Washington, D.C. admitted more than nine million visitors during its first two years of operation. Other regional aerospace museums have sprung up and are continually filled with people and their children who come to see and to wonder at and to be proud of American space accomplishments. Americans have begun to turn their thoughts to the freedom of outer space as evidenced by the extreme popularity of a TV series and movie called *Star Trek* as well as *Star Wars* and others.

But at the same time, proud though they may be, Americans are somewhat hesitant to support a national space program funded out of their tax dollars when there appear to be other, more immediate problems requiring the application of these tax dollars. They pragmatically begrudge a few billion dollars for a limited space program which, as far as they are concerned, amounts to no more than a special group of superbly trained, physically outstanding jet pilots— accompanied by research scientists probing the deep secrets of the universe—taking the most glorious out-of-this-world trips and pursuing their hobbies in the bargain.

This kind of thinking is really the result of some extremely biased reporting by "experts" and "science reporters" in the various news media. These media people were and are journalists who feel they must have a news story full of conflict, danger, and excitement. The space program to date, with few exceptions, has been a big bore to these media people. The space program has been so carefully engineered and operated that even the first trip to the Moon occurred without incident within a few seconds of exactly when it was scheduled. Some media people cannot understand this because they can neither balance their checkbooks nor meet a deadline without turning it into an overtime operation. They would rather report murders, death, famine, revolutions, disasters both natural and human, and other human tragedies . . . and if the story isn't exciting enough, they'll *make* it exciting. It attracts more viewers, listeners, and readers which, in turn, attracts more advertising revenue. The status of honest science reporting in America is grim; all the good science reporters in America would fit comfortably in a Volkswagen Rabbit. And most American newspapers carry such regular features as a complete sports section and a daily astrology column, but never a regular column on science and technology! I've been over the course; I know.

In spite of this, Americans in general sense that there is something more to the space program. We are still very close in time and reality to the frontier that dominated our national consciousness for nearly two centuries. The open, free, frontier culture of America placed a premium on pragmatic people who could face reality and take action. We know what a frontier is; we were just there a few years ago. We sense another one today.

Exploration of a new frontier has always been an acceptable activity worthy of the expenditure of tax revenues—*provided* that what is learned can be translated into a concrete accomplishment of something that needs doing and that a free person who takes the risk can profit from.

What has *not* been reported in the news media and explained widely by reporters and advocates alike is the simple fact that the Solar System—space beyond the Earth's atmosphere—is *not* just a place for exploring, but a place with valuable characteristics and resources that we can *use* to provide products and services of value to others, permitting us to make a profit and a return on investment doing it.

The march of civilization across the centuries has proceeded through those cultures and civilizations whose structure offered the greatest rewards to those individuals who took the maximum risks and succeeded in producing something of value in the process.

To quote historians Will and Ariel Durant from their book, *The Lessons of History:*

"The experience of the past leaves little doubt that every economic system must sooner or later rely upon some form of the profit motive to stir individuals and groups to productivity. Substitutes like slavery, police supervision, or ideological enthusiasm prove too unproductive, too expensive, or too transient. Normally and generally, men are judged by their ability to produce."

The space enterprise will differ in degree—but not in kind—with all of the great ventures of the past. There is one exception: It's going to happen a hundred miles over our heads in space where it hasn't happened at all until very recently. We're now in the process of taming another new frontier, one that we have been exploring for less than 50 years. There is a lot of exploring still to be done, but that shouldn't keep us from using what we have already explored.

Progress in any new frontier breaks down into three phases that overlap one another somewhat but are nonetheless sequential. One phase must always follow its precursor. In the vernacular, "you've gotta touch second base."

The first phase is *exploration*. We go out to the frontier and find out what is there. Usually, we miss the most important long-term implications. For example, Lewis and Clark walked right over the incredible mineral wealth of the American West without suspecting that it was there at all. They were only interested in the physical and geographical characteristics of the frontier. But they blazed the trails where the trappers, hunters, prospectors, miners, farmers, merchants, tradesmen, gamblers, and others eventually followed.

Typically, the exploration phase is financed by a governmental institution using tax revenues. Sometimes it is a government exploration party that goes out; sometimes it's a group of private individuals supported by grants, loans, or other subsidies from the government. This has happened over and over and over again in the past 50 centuries. Commerce has always been the motive, and profit has been the incentive. This was best summarized by President Thomas Jefferson who justified his support of Lewis and Clark to Congress thus:

"The interests of commerce place the principal object within the constitutional powers and care of Congress, and that it should incidentally advance the geographic knowledge of our own continent cannot but be an additional gratification."

In the past 25 years, the United States government through the National Aeronautics and Space Administration (NASA) has explored the space frontier. These exploration efforts have measured and sampled Earth-Moon orbital space; photographed, sampled and mapped the Moon; looked down on Earth from the vantage point of "high orbital ground"; and landed 12 men on the surface of the Moon. Reaching further, we have sent unmanned robot explorers to the planets Mercury, Venus, Mars, Jupiter, and Saturn; probes are now enroute to Uranus and Neptune. Two of our robot explorers have landed on and sampled Mars; the Soviets and the USA have landed probes on Venus.

These achievements in space exploration have been financed at costs that seem modest in comparison to contemporary social programs that have produced questionable results. They have shown that this new frontier in space is a useful frontier. The explorations have proved that the Solar System is a place that can be used by people to solve the problems of people; it can be used to improve the lives of ourselves and our children. Space has become a place in which we can work, live, and engage in profitable activities—i.e., activities that produce things or services of value to us.

We know that orbital space offers a unique place from which to look upon the Earth, affording a view of as much as half the planet in one sweep.

We know that space is a unique environment with valuable industrial characteristics such as weightlessness, hard vacuum, and a wide temperature range.

We know that the Solar System contains a very large and reasonably constant long-term nuclear energy source, the Sun, whose output can be tapped in space to supply the energy needs of people on Earth.

We know that the Solar System contains other planets and celestial bodies such as planetoids and even comets that possess valuable metals and mineral resources. We are still exploring to discover how much of what is located where. We have the technology to utilize these raw materials and thereby to bring to a near-halt the current need to rip them from the surface of our planetary home.

We know that space is a place that we can go to and return from safely. Ten to 15 years from now, travel to and from space need be no more expensive or difficult than crossing the Atlantic Ocean today.

We know that the things that we have done in space up to now have had an incalculable effect upon people living everywhere on this planet. From this, we can reasonably and logically deduce that the further utilization of space will have greater and more significant national and international impact upon economics, education, lifestyles, and standards of living—and all for the better, if we wish to make them that way.

We know that space is not only "the final frontier," but the limitless frontier. This was perhaps best summarized in 1964 by the late pioneer futurist, Dandridge M. Cole:

"Space is a sea without end which washes on countless strange and exotic shores: where the conceivable forms of the living and the dead are greatly outnumbered by the inconceivable; where the known is lost in the unknown; where new dangers hide in undiscovered shadows in unimagined forms; where new goals can challenge and new beauty and wonder can inspire the spirits of all people for all time."

Space is no more of a hostile environment than the

tropical rain forests of the Amazon Valley, the parched
desert of the Sahara, or the snow-swept barrens of the
North Slope of Alaska. It differs only in kind, not degree, from the Great Wilderness faced by the citizens
of the Thirteen Colonies, a wilderness that started only
a hundred miles west of their growing sea coast cities.
The final frontier begins only a hundred miles over our
heads. And it is waiting for anyone who wishes to take
the risks, expend the capital and energy, and do the
work necessary to get out there and use it.

For more than 20 years, we have stumbled into
space without really saying all of the above things in
simple language and telling us *why* we were spending
"all that money" to explore space. Now we know why,
and this news must be communicated.

We are going into space because we need to do it,
because it is a useful thing to do, and because by so
doing we will make a better life for ourselves and our
children.

These are the same reasons why our ancestors left
Europe or Asia to come to the New World and why
they left their reasonably comfortable sea coast cities
to face the hazards and the promise of the Great Wilderness, the Western frontier.

This is why the second phase of space activity which
follows *exploration* is *utilization*, the profitable use of
the unique advantages of space for providing services,
products, and energy to people on Earth and, in the
years to come, to people living in space. The potential
of the utilization of space—space industrialization—
is staggering and has been amply confirmed by numerous independent studies carried out by some of the
best creative, future-oriented people of our time.
Within the lifetimes of most of you reading these
words, space industrialization can provide most if not

all of the raw materials and energy we will need to support a vastly improved lifestyle for *everyone* here on Earth, as well as for the Solar System civilization that is about to begin. This amounts to a new industrial revolution and the next phase of a social growth process that began about 10,000 years ago at the beginning of the Neolithic Age, when people first began to utilize agriculture and huddle together in permanent villages. It is the subject of this book. And it leads inevitably to the third and final phase of space activity.

This third activity, the human *habitation* of space, cannot take place on a large scale and on a permanent basis until space industrialization is established to the point where it requires the presence of large numbers of human beings in space to conduct the activities of space industrialization. Although Soviet cosmonauts are already living in space aboard *Salyut-6* for months at a time in a continuous relay of people back and forth between the space station and Baikonur Cosmodrome, and although we will continue to see increasing numbers of human beings living in space for months or years at a time beginning in the 1980 decade, such limited human habitation of space cannot be considered to be the full-blown human settlement or colonization of space. But such limited living in space is the precursor of the great outrushing of human life in the Great Diaspora which will create the Solar System civilization of the 21st Century. The space colonies will come to pass. But we must touch second base first. The advocates of space colonization have done an admirable job of convincing people that space is useful; and the space colonization advocates have now realized that space industrialization is the necessary *raison d'etre* of space colonization.

There is a great deal of misunderstanding and confusion about these three phases of space activity—exploration, utilization, and habitation. In such a situation, it is often enlightening to take the negative approach and point out what these phases are *not*.

Space exploration is *not* the entire scope of space activity now or in the future. Scientific exploration and experimentation in space are *not* the reasons for doing things in space to the exclusion of everything else. People will not long support a government space program based solely upon exploration; no private space program can be expected to be financed for the long-term on the basis of exploration alone. However, we should and must do all of the space exploration that we can afford, including some unique opportunities that may stretch our resources. One of these unique opportunities is a spacecraft visit to Halley's Comet as it swings around the Sun in 1984; it will not return from the depths of the far Solar System for another 74 years.

Space industrialization is *not* many things, too. It is *not* a program or a specific activity. It is *not* new. It is *not* "far-out Buck Rogers stuff" that is 30 to 50 years in the future. It is *not* just a space station. It is *not* just solar power satellites. It is *not* space colonization. It is *not* totally a government program, because, in order to be viable, it must be responsive to the marketplace. As such, it must be brought to fruition by private enterprise—perhaps supported in its early years by government assistance and incentives in a manner similar to many of the large frontier projects of the past.

Space colonization is *not* the next step in space. It is not the reason and justification for doing space industrialization. Space colonization, as presently envisioned, may not even take place in this century; but it

will take place. It will *not* cost billions of dollars of tax
revenues or capital investment in a lump sum . . . or
even in a series of payments stretched out over decades like a bond issue. It will cost *trillions* of dollars,
and we won't even blink an eye; it will have become
necessary, logical, and inevitable because it will be
part of the evolutionary growth of space industrialization as more and more people are needed in space.
Space colonization is an attractive long-term goal.
But in the meantime we must establish space industrialization on a firm, pay-as-you-go basis.

A great deal has been written and said about space
exploration over the past 50 years. It does not require
repeating here because you can read it elsewhere. And
you can hear about it from those media science reporters who haven't caught on to space industrialization
yet and thus report every space flight in the tried-and-
true formula of space exploration reporting (Don't
blame them too much; most of them don't understand
the motives, operations, or even the basic philosophies
of the free–market private enterprise system.)

And in recent years there has been an increasing
amount of interest and speculation in the area of space
colonization and space habitation. It's a very good
thing that some people are thinking hard about something that's going to happen in the future. A great deal
of very good, hard-nosed engineering and design work
has taken place. It is only fair to point out, however,
that far too much space colonization work has been
pure utopian dreaming; historically, there is nothing
really wrong with this if you keep fact and fiction de-
lineated. Similar utopian dreaming heralded the
opening of the new frontiers of the past. Cathay was
once a magical kingdom with great wizards and magic
that were really advanced technology beyond the

comprehension of visitors. Far Araby was a place of jinns, flying carpets, and odalisques ready to do your every bidding. America was a land of milk and honey where the streets were paved with gold and even if they tossed you in jail it was in golden chains. California was the land of perpetual sunshine where it never rained. And the space colony offers us a pastoral existence with trees, grass, grazing livestock, happy farmers, and dancing children eating goat cheese.

Each generation has evolved its own unique utopia.

But opening a frontier is a deadly, difficult, gut-tearing job that requires the very best people that the human race can produce and demands its toll in lives and property. It takes everything you've got—your gold teeth, your other shirt, and your wife's jewelry. It has *never* been an easy proposition, it isn't today, and it never will be. That is the very nature of a frontier. But just because it is deadly and difficult is no reason not to do it. And it will not stop people from trying; some of them will win. To paraphrase Jonas Ingram, a frontier has no place for well-meaning but uneducated losers; a frontier needs tough sons of bitches who will go out there and *win*! You must roll up your sleeves, get to work, make it happen, and perhaps even die in the process.

Are those kind of people still around? Yes, and in surprising numbers. I am honored to have some of them as friends. They are already at work, getting ready for the final frontier.

And they've got a head start on the rest of you.

CHAPTER TWO

At first glance, the industrialization of space appears to be a frightening melange of activities. If you look around you at the industrial complex of the United States and Canada, it seems to be an incredibly complex system . . . and it is. In spite of years of concerted effort, economists have yet to create a suitable, simple, and analogous mathematical model of our industrial base. The closest approximation to the reality of the American industrial system is the outline produced by the Office of Management and Budget of the Executive Office of the President in an available government book titled, "The Standard Industrial Classification Manual." The SIC is perhaps one of the most important tools that has been developed for statistical analysis of the American economy. It defines all industries in accordance with their composition, product, and structure; it covers the entire field of American economic activity.

The SIC breaks American industry down into 12 distinct Divisions such as "Agriculture, Forestry and Fishing, Mining, Construction," etc. Within each of these Divisions is a further breakdown into Major Groups. There are a total of 99 Major Groups in the SIC, and these major groups are further broken down into the "three-digit SIC groups," which are then further dissected into the "four-digit SIC groups." An example of a four-digit SIC group picked at random from the Manual is Industry No. 3423, "Hand and Edge Tools, Except Machine Tools and Hand Saws." Included in this four-digit break-down are companies who manufacture such things as files, pliers, hand shovels, and oyster tongs.

If this can be done for something as large and complex as the American industrial scene, why can't we do it for space industrialization? This would certainly simplify the discussion. We can, but we won't end up with twelve divisions and ninety-nine major groups and thousands of four-digit groups. The space enterprise can be broken down into major areas that can be briefly summarized as follows:

Communications is the continuing and increasing use of new and improved communications satellites and multi-use space platforms such as orbiting antenna stations to provide more extensive and complete communication between people and between data management systems (computers). Because of the "high view" of Earth that can be obtained from such Earth orbit, the communications area also includes such services as weather satellites, Earth resources satellites, cloud mapping satellites, Earth mapping satellites, navigation satellites, emergency locator satellites, and satellites for tracking individual transmitters on the Earth's surface.

Manufacturing encompasses the field of making new and improved materials that can be made only in the vacuum and weightlessness of space, or materials that can be made better in space because of these unique characteristics. These space characteristics either cannot be duplicated on the ground—weightlessness is an example—or are extremely complex and expensive to obtain on the ground—very high vacuums are an example of that. Initially, space manufacturing will concentrate on unique space-made materials because of the high cost of space transportation. However, as time progresses and space transportation technology matures, the cost will come down. This will permit us to make more and more things in space. Eventually, we will be able to move into space all of our heavy, polluting, energy-consuming industries such as steel mills. Within a century, it will be possible to make in space almost everything that we now make on the ground, plus some things that cannot be made at all here. Furthermore, it will be cheaper, easier, and healthier to do it in space.

Energy involves collecting energy in space—solar energy, for example—for use by space industries *and* for use on Earth. Included in this area is the concept of the solar power satellite first discussed by Dr. Peter E. Glaser of Arthur D. Little, Inc. in 1968. The solar power satellite (SPS) has been the subject of intensive studies by NASA, the Department of Energy, and private industry. Several technical approaches have been looked into: collecting solar energy by either solar cells (photovoltaic) or mirrors, converting solar energy into electricity, beaming the electricity to the ground by microwaves or by lasers, or directly beaming the sunlight to the ground by mirrors. Within 20 years of the "start" signal that would begin the actual experimentation in space and the construction of pilot plants, we could have more than 50 SPS units in orbit around Earth, each supplying 10 gigawatts (10,000,000,000 watts) of electricity. Furthermore, this could be done without the air pollution and carbon-14 radioactivity from coal-fired power plants and without the need for nuclear fission power plants on Earth. Other energy sources in space may also be exploited, including putting fast-breeder nuclear reactors out there where they cannot possibly harm people on Earth. It will also be possible to beam more solar energy directly to the ground where solar conversion panels on housetops could provide us with additional solar power. Finally, there is always the outside chance that we could develop a new source of energy in space such as the matter-anti-matter system. One thing is certain: to increase our energy supplies, we are going to have to go into space to utilize the energy available there; it is becoming more expensive and anti-social to do it here on Earth . . . and it's going to get worse in that respect.

Materials becomes an overriding factor in space industrialization because of the continuing high cost of lifting new materials for industrial processes up from the Earth into space. No matter how efficient we make our future rockets or whether we can manage to develop a new means of propulsion such as a true space drive, no space planner today can foresee the possibility of reducing the lift costs from Earth to orbit below $5 per pound. When your current product costs about $1 per pound made here on Earth, you cannot think about doing it in space at all. However, the Solar System contains abundant raw materials for our industrial base in space. Furthermore, it is cheaper to get such raw materials as iron from the planetoids or titanium from the Moon than it is to haul it up through Earth's strong gravity well. The use of extraterrestrial materials will bring about a turning point in space industrialization because it will reduce costs by a factor of ten or more, just because of the cheaper transportation costs that require less energy. Once space industry has gained its first profitable foothold in the Earth-Moon system in the 1990 decade, and once space transportation costs come down—as transportation costs have historically done in all other transportation areas—we will begin to utilize extraterrestrial materials.

People become an important space activity once the cost of space transportation comes down as a result of industrial needs and technical progress. Lower-cost space transportation is a real economic need for the development of the preceding four areas of space industrialization; the prodding of the marketplace is certain to establish the push to design, build, and operate cheaper means to get into space. To a small extent, this has already happened because of the repetitive cries from industry that current space transportation costs are too high. Initially, people in space will be there to operate the space industrial facilities because there is only so much that automation can accomplish. Engineers are hesitant to automate any industrial process until they understand it well. Early space processes will be so new and so different because of the unique space environment that engineers will want to be on the spot to make adjustments, "tweak" the equipment, and engage in the little, delicate adjustments and fiddling that *always* accompanies putting *any* new industrial process machine into production. These early space industrial engineers will soon be followed by other people who will provide services, running the general store, the medical clinic, and the laundry. Hot on their heels will come other people to produce entertainment in space, taking advantage of the weightless condition of space to make movies, TV shows, and even pornographic films. There will be new types of sports events conducted in weightlessness, a factor that adds a whole new dimension to sporting contests. And as the cost of space transportation to orbit drops to $25 per pound to orbit and return, amounting to a ticket cost of $5,000 or less, tourists will follow. The tourist trade into Earth orbit can be large. Studies have shown that once the cost drops to $10 per pound, it can be as large as transoceanic travel, and current market forecasts estimate that there could be as many as 50,000 tourists per year willing to buy a ticket to orbit once the cost drops to around $1,000.

Putting all these industries and commercial operations in space creates a host of other activities to support them. The space enterprise is broad and extensive, requiring more than simple space factories or planetary launch pads; even on Earth today, a large industrial complex has a town or city to support it. It will also happen in space, and it will form the basis for the space colonies that many people dream of.

There will be something for everyone in space industrialization.

And it will have a profound effect upon Joe Jones, the Man On The Street.

The timing of these five areas of space industrialization is of interest, because it isn't going to happen all at once. There is a definite, logical sequence to it.

This logical sequence of space industrialization may turn out to be a poor forecast, however, and please keep that in mind. We are dealing with a very large and very complex system when we speak of space industrialization. Right now, the logical sequence appears to be the way things will probably go because of risks, capital requirements, and state-of-the-art in technology. But it could change overnight and go some other way. We have had a prime example of this over the past 20 years in the manned space flight area:

If you had asked any space advocate or space planner in 1952-1955 how was the best way to go to the Moon, the answer was the same from everyone: First build a manned space station in orbit around the Earth, then go to the Moon from the space station. It didn't happen that way. Because of a purely political decision and because of purely political considerations, we went directly to the Moon, bypassing the space station step. However, it is interesting to note that we had to come back and touch second base; we had to do the space station step and will probably have to follow through with one or more space stations before we return to the Moon as space industrialists.

So this sequential forecast could be far wide of the mark . . . but here goes:

Communications is an area of space industrialization that is already in existence. It works. It is profitable. It has produced a return on investment. It pays dividends. As I write this, I am looking at my regular Comsat dividend check amounting to 57.5 cents per share. Other companies besides the government-chartered Comsat now believe that space communications is a worthwhile risk and a profitable venture. AT&T, Western Union, and a conglomerate known as Satellite Business Systems are now in the space communications business. Space communications began in the 1960s with the launch of *Telstar*. It proved itself to be profitable in the 1970s. It is going strong now, and the coming decade will see an explosive expansion of communicating capability through comsats of various new sorts.

Manufacturing in space appears to be the thrust of

the 1980 time period, with the early, risky operations being tried out. By 1990, space manufacturing will have become a profitable segment of the space enterprise and will have reached its take-off point. During the first 18 months of Space Shuttle operations scheduled (at this writing) to start in September 1981, 37 payloads have been reserved, including more than 300 small self-contained payloads or "Getaway Specials." These payloads range from a full 32 tons devoted to some sort of space manufacturing experiments aboard the *SpaceLab* in the Shuttle payload bay to the small 200-pound "Getaway Specials" that will fit into empty corners of the payload bay on a space-available basis. A large percentage of these early Shuttle payloads are devoted to development work in space manufacturing, including making new drugs, new alloys, and new electronic semiconductor materials.

The first commercial space products will be sold and used on Earth in the 1980 decade. They will be profitable ventures. Once profitability has been demonstrated, expansion will be extremely rapid as everybody tries to get into the act. To quote one young space industrialist who is already involved, "It's raining soup! Grab a bucket!"

Energy from space is the action of the 1990 decade for several reasons. First of all, one of the big problems with doing anything in Earth orbit is energy; the Space Shuttle Orbiter is sharply limited in electrical power for running experiments and conducting operations; nearly all of its electricity comes from fuel cells where hydrogen and oxygen are brought together to form water and electricity. The development of solar energy systems for space will occupy the activities of many engineers during the first half of the 1980 decade, primarily in building the 25-kilowatt electric power module that will fit into the Shuttle payload bay, unfold its solar panels in space like a butterfly, and provide electrical power for *SpaceLab* experiments. Manufacturing activities in orbit are going to require electric energy, which is probably the easiest and most efficient of all energy forms we currently possess and know how to use. This early work will pave the way for the development, construction, and testing of an SPS "pilot plant" in low-Earth orbit during the latter part of the 1980 decade. This pilot plant will fulfill the function of industrial pilot plants everywhere: checking out the details of new technology. It may produce between 500 megawatts and one gigawatt (a billion watts) of electric power from solar radiation and will test various methods of getting the electricity down to the Earth's surface where it can be switched into existing electric power grids. Some of the methods proposed for transmitting this electric energy include microwave beaming and lasers. The pilot plant will test various approaches. By the 1990 decade, SPS technology will be on its way, and it will require that we build and operate a very large space transportation system and accumulate a large amount of risk capital. By the year 2000, there could be more than 50 SPS units in the geo-stationary or geosynchronous orbit (GSO) 22,200 miles above Earth's surface. This SPS system would supply a major portion of our electric power needs on Earth. Solar energy from space will create as much change in our way of life as did steam power, electricity, and the internal combustion engine.

The 1990 decade will see the beginnings of people in space, thanks to decreased transportation costs. One of the consequences of establishing profitable space manufacturing operations in the 1980s and an SPS system in the 1990s is a large, low-cost space transportation system. This transportation system will be bought and paid for by space manufacturing and space energy. Inexpensive space transportation means 50,000 to 100,000 people in space every year. By the year 2000, the first families will be living in Earth orbit in connection with the space manufacturing facilities and the SPS system. The first decade of the 21st Century will see the beginnings of the Solar System civilization with the first large groups of people living together in space. These will not initially be the huge space colonies with 100,000 people living in them, but smaller space habitats. They may not be located exclusively at the lunar libration points L4 and L5, but wherever large numbers of people are required for the operation of space manufacturing facilities and the SPS system. We can expect to see something resembling the space colony concepts of today after 2010, and they will evolve in Earth orbit from necessity.

By the year 2000, we will have built the space transportation capability and developed the long-term life support technology that will permit us to go back to the Moon and out to the planetoids in search of not only knowledge, but of raw materials. It is already abundantly evident from several studies—as the old space pioneers themselves predicted, by the way—that once you start thinking about doing things and building things in space in a big way, it is cheaper and more efficient if you use extraterrestrial materials from the rest of the Solar System. It is expensive to haul thousands and thousands of tons of material up from the Earth's surface because of Earth's strong gravity field. It is cheaper in terms of energy to get the materials from the Moon with a gravity field one-sixth that of Earth or from the planetoid belt where there is no gravity field at all to speak of. To do this, you must have a space transportation system and you must have some means of providing life support for people over long periods of time. These two items will come from the 1990 decade and the maturing of space manufacturing and the SPS system construction. The first decade of the 21st Century will see people tentatively venturing to the Moon and later to the planetoids. The second decade will undoubtedly find people on the Moon and out in the planetoid belt in large numbers. Beyond those immediate goals lies the possibility of using Martian materials and mining the moons and upper atmosphere of the planet Jupiter in the third decade of the 21st Century.

Within the next 50 years, we can fully expect to find thousands of people living and working in space. They will be operating fantastically complex and advanced space facilities to provide products and services to people on Earth. More than 75% of these products do not exist today. They will be providing billions of dollars of return on investment to people such as you and me who have invested a few hard-earned dollars in these new space ventures. Even people of the Third World nations will benefit from the space enterprise; because it is supranational it will affect planet Earth as a single entity.

The most important factor to keep in mind about the space enterprise is that it "opens up the system." There have been many serious studies of the future that have come to the conclusion that Earth is finite in size, in resources, and in its capabilities to support and sustain life. These studies have confirmed what many of us have known for a long time. But it required the psychological shock of the Apollo photographs of our planet hanging like a blue-white ball against the

blackness of space. These photos drove home the fact
that the Earth is finite. It scared the living hell out of
most people because Earth seems such an immense
place when you have to walk around on its surface and
can see only a few square miles at a time. These studies
have caused many people, including some futurists
and forecasters who should know better, to flip into
complete panic and call for an immediate halt to
everything having to do with technology, progress,
etc. They would have us go back to the cave. What they
do not realize is that without technology and an incredible use of natural energy, Earth will support perhaps only 10 million people. We cannot go backwards.
If Closed System Earth has limits to our growth, and
if we face the prospect of stagnating and decaying in
our own garbage, we'd better think about opening up
the system.

The concept is analogous to an unborn baby in the
eighth month of pregnancy. The womb is beginning to
get crowded. Waste products are removed less quickly
and sometimes have a tendency to build up far beyond
previous levels. If the baby could forecast, it would
come to the conclusion that things are going to get
limited very quickly. In the ninth month, it runs out of
room to expand. In the tenth month, things become
impossible. There is some indication of a larger universe because of sounds and motion and pressures on
the womb. But the unborn baby knows nothing of this.
It only appears that things are going to get very bad
indeed and that there is a limit to growth. Growth cannot go on under those conditions in that closed system.
And it doesn't. The system is suddenly opened up. The
baby is born into a much larger system.

We are in the process of being born into the universe.
The space enterprise is the way we are going to be

born and the way we are going to support ourselves and our growth in the future.

So much for the philosophical background. What are the realities?

There is work to be done. There are great challenges to be met. There are go-for-broke gambles to be made. There are fortunes to be made. And there are new and horrible ways to die. A frontier is always that way, and this new frontier a hundred miles over our heads is no different. It is waiting for us to come and use its fantastic potential.

In 25 years many of the fantastic statements, forecasts, and predictions made in this book will be looked upon with a chuckle because they will have turned out to be hopelessly conservative and lacking in foresight.

However, I present here what we *could* do. The scenario of the space enterprise taken all by itself and not considering any of its interactions with possible world scenarios can be broken down as follows into these ten-year phases:

1980—1990: Communications continues to improve its technology and profitability. *Manufacturing* development work begins, leading to initial profitability by the decade's end. *Energy* enters developmental work leading to a pilot SPS system by the decade's end.

1990—2000: Communications and *manufacturing* both continue development, improvement, and profitability during this decade. *Energy* becomes the leading activity with the large-scale construction and online operation of an SPS system with as many as 50 units by the decade's end. *People* are beginning to become an important space activity due to the SPS system, and space tourism is just beginning at the decade's end.

2000—2010: Communications, manufacturing, and

energy are all activities that are improving and profitable. *People* becomes the activity of the decade with increasing numbers of people required for in-space activities and a rapidly expanding space tourism activity. Initial prospecting of the Moon and the planetoids for extraterrestrial (ET) *materials* begins in order to reduce costs.

2010—2020: The space enterprise is in full bloom with *communications, manufacturing, energy, people,* and ET *materials* as going profitable operations. There is no question at this future time as to the risk, return on investment, or track record. The Solar System civilization is well started. More and more people are required in space to make it happen. And the first large space habitats with 10,000 people or more are beginning to take form.

This is a solidly-based forecast erring perhaps on the conservative side. It could happen faster than this if the 1980 decade shows that both manufacturing *and* energy are needed and profitable operations, thereby causing some push on space transportation systems with a consequent lowering of space transportation costs. A worst case situation (to be discussed in detail in a later chapter) shows that this forecast will be delayed at most by only 20 to 25 years by a failure of American nerve or will or by cyclical economic factors. Only a planetary catastrophe such as an all-out thermonuclear war between superpowers might stop it entirely, and even this is questionable.

The space enterprise is almost as certain as tomorrow's sunrise.

CHAPTER THREE

Communications is the one area of the space enterprise in the 1970 decade that has what every banker, financial planner, businessman, industrialist, and manager looks for in a venture: a proven track record.

It's a matter of "ho hum."

Twenty years ago, it wasn't.

According to Robert A. Heinlein, there is nothing as commonplace as a 90–day wonder on the 91st day.

By taking a closer look at the communications area of the space enterprise, how it started, where it has been, where it is today, and where it can go tomorrow, we can get a better grasp of the total space enterprise picture.

The title of space communications prophet belongs to Arthur C. Clarke, a founder and past-chairman of the British Interplanetary Society who, during World War II, was connected with the development and testing of what is called in aviation today "precision approach radar." At the end of World War II, they called it "ground controlled approach." Thus, Clarke was familiar with both modern electronics and the burgeoning field of rocketry and astronautics. Clarke wrote a popular scientific article entitled "Extra-terrestrial Relays" that appeared in the October 1945 issue of the

British magazine, *Wireless World*. (I am privileged to have an autographed reprint of the original article.)

And it was another science-fiction author who wrote under the pen-name of J.J. Coupling who made it happen. In real life, this science-fiction writer was Dr. John R. Pierce of Bell Laboratories in New Jersey. Pierce forecast that American Telephone and Telegraph Company (AT&T) could save as much as four billion dollars per year on the maintenance of long-line telephone networks on the ground in the 1950s if there was a communications satellite in orbit to handle that traffic.

Although the passive communications satellite *Echo-I* went into orbit on August 12, 1960 and the first active communications test satellite called *Courier-I* went up on October 4, 1960, the first commercial communications test satellite *Telstar-I* was orbited on July 10, 1962. *Telstar-I* was built and its launching by NASA was paid for by AT&T. And the man in charge was Dr. John R. Pierce. *Telstar-I* proved that Clarke's idea would work because it transmitted data like television programs, photographs, and newspaper front pages.

Telstar-I not only caused a public sensation but a political furor. Who was to own, operate, and control the communications satellite? A contemporary Bill Mauldin cartoon shows *Telstar-I* transmitting the message, "If it works, the government owns it!" Actually, the United States government is a signatory to numerous telecommunications treaties and participates in worldwide telecommunications conferences and committees to regulate radio transmissions, assign radio frequencies, and determine amounts of charge and method of payment for telecommunications services. The communications satellite was a whole new wrinkle in the world telecommunications picture. Some technique had to be developed that would bring the communications satellite and the potential of communications satellite networks within the provisions of various international treaties.

Several proposals for the ownership and regulation of communications satellites were introduced in both houses of Congress. The Senate Committee on Aeronautical and Space Sciences reported out one such bill, and the Senate passed it . . . but not without 20 days of debate, including a filibuster from liberal senators who wanted full government ownership of the whole system. The House of Representatives turned down the Senate bill and, on August 27, 1962, passed H.R.11040 under suspension of the House rules permitting changes in conference committee with the Senate. On August 31, 1962, President John F. Kennedy signed into law the Communications Satellite Act of 1962.

The result was a new, government chartered corporation, Communications Satellite Corporation (Comsat), to be a government-regulated but privately owned corporation. In a unique arrangement, communications companies such as AT&T, General Telephone, ITT, and others were permitted to purchase and own up to 50% of the common stock of Comsat. The remaining 50% of the common stock was offered to the general public in the amount of 5,000,000 shares at a price of $20 per share. A total of $200 million in equity capital was raised from 130,000 shareholders within a matter of weeks in July 1964. More than half (65,000) of the initial shareholders owned from 11 to 50 shares of Comsat stock, while 52,000 people owned from one to 10 shares. There were shareholders in every one of the 50 states, the District of Columbia, and Puerto Rico.

This tells us something about interest in the future of the space enterprise: The American public is willing to support and invest their hard-earned money in a space venture if there is a reasonable chance of getting a return on investment and making some money in the process. Comsat proved that in 1964. We need to remember this 15 years later, when people talk about a "public disenchantment with space." According to the Comsat Annual Report for 1978, there are still 83,428 stockholders and 52 common carrier companies holding stock in Comsat.

Comsat spent its equity capital on a series of constantly improved larger communications satellites and on an expanding system of ground stations.

It wasn't until October 16, 1970 that the Comsat Board of Directors declared the first dividend of 12.5 cents per share. That is approximately $1 million and represents a milestone: the first money made by the general public from a space enterprise. But it is not and will not be the last. Comsat now pays an annual dividend of $2.30 per share.

It took a little over six years for Comsat to go from initial start-up to a dividend-paying operation.

As expected, changes have occurred in Comsat over the years. It is now the general managing agent of Intelsat, an international consortium of 102 nations. NASA still launches the communications satellites for Comsat, but the satellites are now bigger, heavier, more complex, and called *Intelsat*. It also operates a maritime communications satellite system called *Marisat* and a domestic system called *Comstar*.

There are two elements of competition for Comsat and Intelsat. One is semi-competitive, the communications satellite system of the USSR that was set up to compete with Intelsat in August 1968. The Soviets originally called it *InterSputnik* and invited other socialist and communist nations to participate. They used their *Molniya* communications satellites. The venture was not successful, but the USSR's *Orbita* domestic comsat program was. And now the USSR is inviting others to join the *Orbita* system. There is even some indication that the Soviets may join Intelstat, if the United States will back down from its controlling position.

The success of Comsat has prompted other firms to get into the business . . . as might certainly be expected in a free but highly regulated marketplace. AT&T is back in the satellite business with *Comstar D-2* launched on July 22, 1976 to expand Ma Bell's U.S. communications system. Western Union has a comsat in orbit. Satellite Business Systems was formed as a partnership between Comsat General, Aetna Life & Casualty, and IBM to provide a system for large companies and the government with substantial and innovative internal voice, data, and video communications services.

What is success in space communications? Comsat's 1978 operating revenues were more than $184 million, with a net income of more than $34 million. *That* is success!

What is to come? A great deal, and it will be distinctly different from what has occurred in space communications to date.

To grasp this difference, one must be aware of a new phenomenon called "complexity inversion." It is a very simple concept that holds the key to greatly expanded capabilities in space.

Up until now, space payloads such as communication satellites have been launched into orbit by converted military strategic rocket vehicles or boosters

derived from military ICBM programs. Because of the
weight limitations of these military rockets, originally
designed to lob thermonuclear warheads halfway
around the world, satellite payload weights have been
sharply limited. Using the biggest and most expensive
converted military launch vehicles such as the Atlas-
Centaur and the Titan-IIIC, it is possible to put about
5,000 pounds of satellite into the "geosynchronous"
orbit 22,200 miles above the equator—a prime site for
comsats because they go around the Earth in 24 hours,
thus appearing to stand still in the sky when seen from
the ground. The amount of power that could be put
into a satellite in the form of batteries was limited by
weight, and the amount of solar energy generated by
solar cell panels on the satellite was also limited by
both weight and size restraints. Add to these restrictions the fact that, once launched, there is absolutely
no way to call it back and fix it if something goes
wrong. Therefore, this highly limited payload must
contain redundant or multiple elements to insure that
it is going to work, and the payload must undergo extensive and rigorous testing on the ground before
launch. All of this costs money. And if the satellite
quits in orbit, it must be written off the books and a
new satellite must be put up in its stead.

These restrictions mean that engineers must design
very small, very lightweight, and very reliable components for current satellites. Insofar as possible, all
the complexity, size, weight, and heavy energy-de-
mand must be designed into the ground-based portion
of the system, resulting in very large and expensive
Earth stations.

The coming of the NASA Space Shuttle has changed
all of this. The Shuttle Orbiter can carry as much as
65,000 pounds into low-Earth orbit and do this once a

week on a regular schedule. Size is no longer a constraint; the Orbiter payload bay is more than 60 feet long and 15 feet in diameter.

Think of it another way. The next time a big semi-trailer truck blasts past you on the highway, take a good look at it. The entire rig—tractor, trailer, and load—will fit into the Orbiter's payload bay and can be lofted into space every Thursday morning! Or consider the fact that the Space Shuttle Orbiter's payload bay will accommodate and orbit a loaded railway box car.

With this orbital weight-lifting capability added to the fact that the Orbiter can carry the satellite into space where people can check it out in the space environment before committing it to orbit, the satellites can not only get bigger and heavier, but also more complicated. After all, if the Orbiter crew checks out the satellite and finds that something didn't survive the flight into orbit or isn't working in space, they simply close the payload bay doors and return the failing satellite to Earth so it can be fixed. With the assistance of an "upper stage" carried in the payload bay, the satellite can be boosted into geosynchronous orbit. As the 1980 decade progresses, a *manned* orbital transfer vehicle (OTV) will come into use, permitting people to accompany the satellite all the way to its operating orbital station. The manned capability to travel regularly to geosynchronous orbit carries with it another important consequence: satellites in orbit can be visited to make repairs or can be taken out of orbit, returned to Earth, fixed, and put back into space again.

This now means that it is possible to put very large, very complex, and very powerful satellites in orbit while the ground stations to work with the satellites become very small, very inexpensive, and very simple.

This is what is meant by complexity inversion, and it is forcing satellite designers to completely change the way they design and build satellites: In the future, the big, powerful, and expensive stuff is in space while the simple, small, and inexpensive equipment is on the ground.

This is going to make a big difference.

Future comsats will be able to pick up the signal from a "wee-watter" transmitter on Earth—one broadcasting with less than one watt or, at most, only a few watts like today's CB walkie-talkies. Because the satellite has lots of transmitting power, it can also send a signal back to the ground that can be picked up with a simple whip antenna on a hand-held, battery-operated receiver. The possibility of orbiting very large satellites also means that they will have the capability to handle thousands and thousands of individual radiotelephone voice circuits as well as dozens of TV channels . . . on top of hundreds of data transfer channels where computers talk to one another.

With big antennas in space, some of them miles long, it will also be possible for the satellite to locate with great accuracy any transmitter signaling it from the Earth below.

Furthermore, because the available locations in geosynchronous orbit are becoming crowded—there are several hundred operating satellites out there in orbit 22,200 miles above the Earth, and most of them are grouped together in prime locations such as that over the equator between Brazil and Africa—the numerous individual satellites devoted to one specific type of service can be combined into one very large Geosynchronous Communications Platform. Dr. Walter Morgan of Comsat Laboratories has called this concept the "Orbiting Antenna Farm," or OAF for short.

Combined in a single Geosynchronous Communications Platform (GCP) would be the following services:

Direct broadcast television: Right now, earth-based TV reception requires that the receiver be within line of sight of the transmitter. Satellite-relayed TV eliminates this line–of–sight requirement. But since we are still on the "back side" of complexity inversion, very large and expensive ground stations are required to utilize the service. The large GCP will make it possible to pick up TV programs directly relayed from the satellite using nothing more than a simple antenna and a frequency converter. This will bring TV to areas where it does not exist today or must be brought in by cable. One single GCP could provide five simultaneous color TV channels and cover the entire continental U.S.

The wrist radio and pocket telephones: The Dick Tracy wrist radio becomes a reality with the large GCP, although because of battery technology the original units may have to be as large as a walkie-talkie radio or a belt paging beeper. The initial GCP would have only 45,000 individual channels which could be used from any portable telephone within sight of the satellite and, through the satellite, could be connected to any other portable telephone or into the existing telecommunications network here and abroad. The initial cost would be about $300 for the unit and about $3.00 per call, but these costs would drop steadily over a ten-year period to about $30 per unit and 30 cents per call, based upon the analogies of the hand calculator and CB market histories. Within 20 years—or by the end of the century—there could be as many as 50 million users with annual revenues from calls alone exceeding $20 billion. The equipment market exceeds $150 million per year within ten years of the introduction of the service.

National information service: How would you like your town or college library to have available for you the entire contents of the Library of Congress and the New York City Public Library . . . at a simple data console with a small three-foot parabolic antenna on the roof of the building and an inexpensive box of electronics? It's possible with the GCP. Or how would you like to have one of these gadgets in your office to gain access to the latest data or to interface with extremely large general purpose computers located elsewhere? And all of this for a reasonable cost? The local data console, electronic converter, and antenna puts you in direct contact with the GCP in orbit, which is, in turn, linked with very large library computers as well as very large general purpose computers. Studies have shown that there are about 20,000 libraries in the USA that could and would use this service, but that there are probably at least *two million business firms* that would want such a service. This will change the book publishing industry beyond all recognition, and probably also cause great changes in newspaper and magazine publishing because you will be able to get it all via satellite . . . and eventually in your own home. (There are a number of science writers and science-fiction writers today who are fortunate to already have computer terminals in their homes.) This service is going to make money, and it will make all communications satellite revenues to date seem like small change. By ten years after the service is initiated, the most conservative estimates put revenues at more than $5 billion per year.

Teleconferencing: This is already going on, and it will grow if energy becomes more expensive and thus impacts business travel. The objective is to sit in your conference room in Los Angeles and, through TV and audio links, hold a "face-to-face" conference with somebody in a similar conference room in New York City. It's being done today by Rockwell International between their Space Systems Division in Downey, California and their corporate headquarters in Pittsburgh, Pennsylvania. It is an expensive service today because of the large bandwidth and number of channels required in a land-based system. However, by doing it through a large satellite with a large number of channels and lots of bandwidth, costs come down significantly. The GCP originally would handle audio-video links from as many as 300 ground sites simultaneously. As the service grows and the technology progresses, it will become possible to transmit holographic images through the satellite communications link, so instead of watching the remote conference members on a TV screen, their holographic image will be projected right into your conference room, and they will appear to be sitting right across the table from you—although they are, in reality, perhaps on the other side of the world.

Electronic mail: The world still runs on hard copies, and the business in the teletype and TWX market is brisk even today. There are gadgets that can be interfaced with an ordinary telephone that will transmit a facsimile of any written or printed document across the country or around the world on existing telephone systems—but it takes a couple of minutes to transmit the data. The Western Union telegram is pretty much a thing of the past, but the WU Mailgram business has shown surprising growth because there is still a need to move a hard copy somewhere else by tomorrow morning. Electronic mail via satellite is one of the services to be installed on the GCP. Personal and business correspondence would be relayed by facsimile through the GCP, and terminals would be in regional postal centers. Each center would contain the equipment required to automatically convert hard copy to facsimile and vice-versa without human surveillance and thus insuring privacy—as much privacy as currently exists with the mails, at any rate. With a single satellite, the GCP electronic mail system would be able to deliver 40 million letter-sized pages from source to destination overnight.

It is vitally important to point out something here: Designs for the GCP exist. The technology to accomplish everything discussed here exists. The markets to support these services exist and have been thoroughly surveyed and studied. The capital requirements to initiate the various services and bring them to break-even are reasonable—ranging from about $200 million up to some $4 billion for electronic mail—with a projected rate of return from 11% to 17% (except for the electronic mail which, in common with most postal services, never achieves break-even).

Everything we are discussing here can come to pass before 1990.

The risk is relatively low, considering the track record of Comsat. The return on investment occurs within ten years and at a reasonable rate of return.

All we have to do is establish the organizations to do it, acquire the equity capital to pay for it, and utilize the NASA Space Shuttle to put it in place. Even by charging exceedingly reasonable rates for the services, you'd better have a good pipeline for deposits to the nearest large bank.

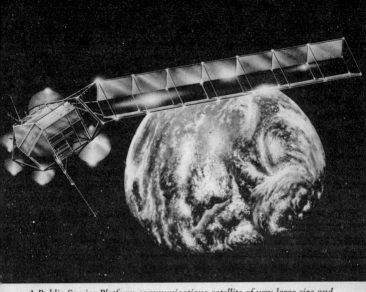

A Public Service Platform communications satellite of very large size and complexity in geosynchronous Earth orbit about 1988. Powered by a solar collector several hundred feet long, the PSP mounts a number of very large and powerful radio, television, and data transmission antennas capable of handling many TV channels as well as wrist radios, library data channels, and business data channels. This design derives from a Rockwell International hardware design study.

Beyond this very early and primitive GCP, there are other things that can be done with communications and data transfer satellites in Earth orbit in the next 20 years.

Did you ever lose a package in shipment? In fact, did you ever lose a whole shipment? It happens all the time, and hundreds of man-hours and thousands of dollars are spent trying to find out why the carton went to Portland, Maine instead of Portland, Oregon or why the boxcar ended up on the siding in East Chitlin Switch, Kansas . . . when you finally do locate the boxcar. As a matter of fact, the American railroads today do not know the location of several thousand of their privately owned freight cars; there just happens to be enough freight cars around that they can get what they need when they need it, regardless of who really owns it. It will be a very easy problem to solve when we put a locator satellite in geosynchronous orbit.

A locator satellite would have two antennas, each about two miles long, in the north-south and east-west orientation in orbit. Reception beams from each antenna would scan back and forth across the United States, one beam scanning from north to south and the other from east to west. On the ground, you have attached a tiny milliwatt radio transmitter made with VLSI chips to your package, and this little transmitter continually sends forth its digitally coded signal saying, "Here I am, and my name is WFRY-09786!" The two satellite scanner beams pick up this signal; one beam locates it north–and–south, and the other east–and–west, and the information is sent back to "locator central" on the ground, where the data is stored in a computer. When the package doesn't arrive on schedule, you query locator central which queries the computer that tells you where it was no later than one hour ago. Such a locator satellite could locate ten billion little transmitters to within 100 feet every hour.

Of course, if such a locator satellite can do that for ten billion packages and shipments, it can also do the very same thing for Junior when he gets lost on the Boy Scout hike. He's got an emergency locator button on his Scout uniform, and his Scoutmaster has a portable telephone. Scoutmaster calls locator central, gives Junior's transmitter code, and satellite tells Scoutmaster where in the trackless wilderness Junior is—plus or minus 100 feet. The same thing can be done for airplanes that get lost, automobiles that get stolen, shipments that get hijacked or ripped off, or people whom the police want to keep track of . . . which again goes to prove that technology is what you make of it. It you want to insure that the locator satellite isn't used by a repressive, totalitarian government, you'd better keep it out from under government control and let it be owned and operated by private enterprise.

One year after you get this locator satellite service into operation, you can probably expect operating revenues from $2.8 million to $8 million. Twelve years later, your revenues could be as much as $300 million, and you've got a company equivalent to Comsat today.

Such a locator satellite combined with the technology of the wrist radio and its associated satellite system, gives you the capability for fantastically accurate navigation and location. Punch the proper button on your wrist computer, and it flashes your latitude and longitude, or the distance from Lattiville, or the direction to the nearest McDonald's.

Using the complexity inversion of future space communications, the things that you can do are limited only by politics and by the delays thrown in your path by competitive systems. You can conduct national polls and elections, locate nuclear fuels, monitor ocean resources, keep trains from running into each other and ships from hitting reefs with cargoes of crude oil aboard.

By the year 2010, a very conservative estimate of the potential revenues possible from only 15 new communications–information services through complexity inversion satellites in the space enterprise would be running at about $47 billion per year.

All this is more than just the beginning of the space enterprise, building upon something with a proven track record that is already there. It is only one area of the space enterprise.

CHAPTER FOUR

The concept of using the characteristics of space for the purpose of making materials and products isn't new. Science-fiction writers, myself included, were writing about such things as long ago as 1950. And some critical and pioneering experiments have already been conducted on several *Apollo* missions, in *Skylab*, and agressively by the Soviets aboard the *Soyuz* and *Salyut* spacecraft. The results of these pioneering experiments are promising. Space offers the industrialist several important physical characteristics as well as some critical social advantages.

Space as an industrial environment exhibits (a) weightlessness or "free fall," a condition in which normal gravitational forces to which we're accustomed on Earth are absent; (b) very high vacuum which is expensive to obtain in large quantities on Earth and must be considered both as a place with nothing in it and also as a place into which you can put anything you want with assurance that only your material is present; (c) very wide temperature ranges all the way from about 4° K. or -269° Celsius up to several thousand degrees C. or F. (because it doesn't make too much difference at those temperatures); and (d) a wide variety of electromagnetic radiation from the Sun ranging from radio waves up to X-rays and gamma rays. All of these four items are in space now; they are waiting to be used for industrial purposes in making things by industrial processes.

Important social attributes also exist. First of all, industrial processes in space pose, for all intents and purposes, absolutely zero pollution problems for the Earth's biosphere. Thus, in time, we can move our heavily polluting industries into space. Since practically all energy for space processing comes from the Sun, it does not further deplete Earth's natural energy resources and, furthermore, cannot possibly add to the Earth's heat load. If we do not like to live with some of the industrial processes we now have on Earth, the obvious solution (since we cannot do without these industrial processes) is to move them somewhere else where they can't bother Earth . . . and into an environment that is actually more benign for industrial processes anyway.

This is the whole basic concept behind the author's original interest in space industrialization. It seemed that there had to be *some* solution to eliminating most industrial pollution on Earth without giving up the valuable advantages of industrialization. These basic concepts are presented in detail in *The Third Industrial Revolution*, available in paperback from Ace Books.

The early experimental work and theoretical analysis of space processing is encouraging. We can make things in space that we cannot make at all here on Earth because of the presence of gravity here; and we can probably make many things in space better than we can make them on Earth for the same reasons. Eventually, we will be able to make in space almost everything that we are presently making here on Earth without the associated Earthly problems.

However, this view isn't shared by everyone, and I want to settle that matter once and for all right now. Then you can make up your mind.

In 1978, the Committee on Scientific and Technological Aspects of Materials Processing in Space of the National Research Council in Washington published a report, "Materials Processing in Space," in which a number of *incredible* statements were made, statements which will join other great pronouncements indicating failure of imagination and/or will:

"The Committee concludes that the prospects for using the space environment for science and technology related to materials processing take the form of incremental advantages over Earth–based processes rather than breakthroughs into new science and technology." The report also states, "The influence of gravity in most phenomena is well known."

This view is echoed by the Chairman of the Committee, William P. Schlicter, in testimony before the House Committee on Science and Technology on May 23, 1979: "The effects of gravity have long been known with great accuracy . . . "

One would certainly think that by this time scientists, technologists, and other "experts" would have learned to be somewhat more cautious about making such statements. Obviously, the Committee was not aware of Arthur C. Clarke's Law: "When a distinguished but elderly scientist states that something is possible, he is almost certainly right. When he states that something is impossible, he is very probably wrong."

And not just elderly scientists, or even scientists, either.

Witness the record of history for a few selected statements similar to Schlicter's dilly:

"You are welcome to use the schoolroom to debate all proper questions; but such things as railroads are impossibilities and rank infidelity. If God had designed that His intelligent creatures should travel at the frightful speed of 15 miles per hour by steam, He would have foretold it through His holy prophets." This denial of permission to hold a seminar came from an Ohio school board in 1828. This was three years after Colonel John Stevens of Hoboken, New Jersey, had an operating steam locomotive running on the lower lawn of his estate there. And 22 years after Richard Trevethick's *Pen-y-darran* locomotive in Wales hauled a load consisting of 10 tons of iron, five wagons, and 70 people.

Well, school boards are not noted for their innovative outlooks nor for their ability to keep abreast of current events. But how about the anonymous British scientist who, in 1815, stated, "A voyage from Liverpool to New York by steam is as impossible as a flight to the Moon!" Score one point against sober scientific forecasting.

Let's get closer to our own time. "The demonstration that no possible combination of known substances, known forms of machinery, and known forms of force can be united in a practical machine by which man shall fly long distances through the air seems to the writer as complete as it is possible for the demonstration of any physical fact to be," stated Professor Simon Newcomb in October 1903, less than 60 days before the first flight of the Wrights at Kitty Hawk, North Carolina; at that time, the Wrights had already built their Flyer and its engine and were in the process of getting it ready to ship to Kitty Hawk.

Another expert holds forth: "Two notions about aviation of the future you may be prepared to discharge—the stratospheric flight for passenger traffic and the 500-miles-per-hour flight." The prophet: aviation pioneer Igor Sikorski as reported in an article by Paul Gallico in the August 1935 *Reader's Digest.*

Testifying before Congress on December 3, 1945, Dr. Vannevar Bush stated in part, "There has been a great deal said about a 3000 mile-high angle rocket . . . In my opinion, such a thing is impossible for many years. I wish the American public would leave that out of their thinking."

These are but a few examples from a rather large file of foolish statements by experts that I maintain as an "Utter Bilge" file whose title is attributable to the famous evaluation of the British Astronomer Royal, Sir Richard van der Riet Wooley, "Space travel is utter bilge."

It seems that Clarke's Law is still at work, and I am very glad that my name is *not* on that NRC report. It takes a tremendous amount of ego, over-education, and total lack of perspective—to say nothing of a complete ignorance of history—to make such presumptuous statements. True, we have much to learn about materials processing in space . . . but we certainly do not know everything there is to know about the effects of gravity on all potential microscopic and macroscopic physical processes. We will learn, and I believe that the HRC statement coupled with Schlicter's quote provide us with a great deal of optimistic probability that we do indeed have something when it comes to making products in space!

One of the big problems with advanced technology today is the fact that some academicians and research scientists want to study everything to death and understand it completely before they are willing to admit that it has utility. Well, their jobs and livelihoods depend upon those research grants and contracts, so don't be too harsh on them. Over the long haul, they do indeed increase our understanding of the universe. But it takes entrepreneurs, industrial engineers, production engineers, quality control people, marketing people, and managers to really do the job . . . and the quality of results they can obtain from exceedingly meager scientific data is surprising. The late Dr. William O. Davis (who was *not* ignorant of Clarke's Law) once pointed out that it is inventors who come up with new things, engineers who translate those things into valuable products, and scientists who then come along to explain how and why it works in the first place.

We already know enough about space environmental conditions and the behavior of certain materials under those conditions to make some pretty good guesses at some of the possible new space products that are likely to come along in the 1980 decade.

The 1980 decade is going to see the beginnings of space products just as the 1960s saw the start of space communications. The first product made in space will be sold and will make a profit in the 1980 decade.

SpaceLab, a modular space laboratory built by a consortium of 10 European nations, will enable people from both academic and industrial research establishments to conduct materials processing experiments in orbit for up to 30 days. They will be able to ride along with their experiments and conduct them in the space environment.

In addition to *SpaceLab*, there are over 300 Small Self Contained Payloads or "Getaway Specials" already reserved by individuals, small companies, schools, and even giant corporate conglomerates. A Getaway Special is limited to 200 pounds in weight and 5 cubic feet in volume. It must fit into a standard NASA-supplied cannister which is fitted into a spare corner of the Space Shuttle Orbiter's 15-foot by 60-foot payload bay on a "payload of opportunity" basis. It must be completely self-contained and require no power or services from the Orbiter. Three on-off switch signals are provided by the flight crew from the Shuttle cabin. Cost: $500 down on application and the balance of $3,000 to $10,000 payable when the Getaway Special flies. More than 300 of these have been reserved, and a great percentage of them will be devoted to materials processing experiments.

Some of the space-made materials under consideration for the experiments are crystals and special alloys.

SkyLab experiments in crystal-growing in space proved that it's possible to grow very large crystals with very few imperfections. Here in Earth's gravity, dislocations of the crystalline lattice caused by gravity limit the size and perfection of crystals. So what? Of what possible use are large crystals grown in space? Are they just a scientific curiosity? Not at all.

The world of modern electronics depends upon crystals with specific amounts of impurities added to form semiconductors—transistors, for example. Most integrated circuit chips are specially grown crystals. The reject rate is fairly high because of crystalline lattice imperfections, and the number of "chips" that can be cut from a single "boule" or crystal is limited by the size of the crystal that can be grown here on Earth. A study by General Electric indicates that the cost of some integrated circuits made from space-grown crystals can be reduced by as much as a factor of ten. This is because of the potential of growing better crystals of larger size in space.

In the absence of gravity, it is also possible to make very thin films of uniform thickness (or thinness) and very large size. Thin films also form one of the foundations of modern integrated circuit technology. Thinner and better films of large size will also reduce the cost and size of integrated circuits while at the same time increasing their performance.

Oil and vinegar salad dressing won't stay mixed here on Earth because gravity causes the lighter oil to rise to the top of the more dense vinegar. But oil and vinegar would stay mixed in the weightlessness of space. There are many other materials that behave the same way. Many of them are mixtures of metals called alloys. Bronze, a mixture of copper and tin, was probably the first alloy made by people. The alloy technology of metallurgical science today is very complex, but there are some alloys that cannot be made here on Earth for the same reason you can't keep oil and vinegar mixed for long. In space, it would be possible to make such alloys with a uniform set of properties.

And it appears possible to make some alloys in space that cannot be made at all here on Earth because, in a gravity field, their constituent materials won't "wet" each other and won't stay mixed at all. For example, gallium arsenide is an alloy of gallium and arsenic that is widely used in the semiconductor industry. The element bismuth is of the same family as arsenic in the Periodic Table of Elements, but it is totally impossible to make gallium bismide on Earth because it will not mix. In the weightlessness of space, it will mix. We do not know what the physical or electronic properties of gallium bismide might be, but they might be very unusual. Within ten years we will know. Whoever makes it in space and perfects the process may also make a lot of money. How much money?

A linear extrapolation of current semiconductor market growth indicates that by the year 2000 the market size will be more than *$12 billion*. Let's take a very conservative estimate. If you could begin making semiconductor materials in orbit by 1985 and could capture a mere 1% of the market, and if you could hold a conservative 1% of the market, you'd make a half-million dollars in 1985 and more than $127 million in 2000 A.D. Obviously, you should be able to do better than this. Semiconductor materials have a very high value, ranging from $250 to $500 per pound. This is just the sort of product whose ultimate value can justify the high space transportation costs that are inevitable in the 1980s; in the 1990s, however, you can anticipate a drastic reduction in these transportation costs.

Because it is possible to grow such good crystals in space, there is also the potential of being able to grow materials that are directionally solidified. A crystal does the same thing—grow in one direction. Other materials can be solidified so that their internal structure is different in one direction than in another. The applications for directionally solidified materials that could be made in space are interesting and profitable.

Some of the initial space processing experiments in directionally solidified materials offer promise of new and improved bearing materials. Wear is perhaps the greatest bearing problem—and if you've ever worn out an automobile engine, this is just one example. If you can make better bearing materials such as balls, races, inserts, sleeves, etc. that have corrosion resistance, high temperature capability, lubricity, and very low creep or propensity to slowly deform under a load, you might be able to capture a sizable portion of the total bearing market which grows from a total of

$4.6 billion in 1985 to $6.9 billion in 2000. A mere, conservative 1% of this market doesn't make you into a Fortune 500 company, but it provides a sizable multi-million-dollar gross sales figure.

The capability to manufacture directionally solidified materials in orbit also permits you to make very good cobalt/rare earth magnets (CORE magnets). These have very cohesive magnetic fields for their size and would permit the manufacture of electrical equipment that would be much smaller and lighter. For example, you could reduce the size and weight of an electric motor by a significant factor while at the same time increasing its energy efficiency. In the 1980s, high-quality magnetic material will bring a price of about $750 per pound, making CORE magnets an attractive potential space product. By 1988, the market for CORE magnets is estimated to be more than $13 million per year rising to as much as $100 million per year by 2000.

Initial space products such as the ones suggested above all exhibit several common characteristics: (a) they have a very high cost per pound which is necessary to offset the high initial transportation costs of Space Shuttle, and (b) they can be made only in space or can be made better in space. With these characteristics in mind, another product suggests itself: perishable cutting tools (PCT). These are the metal cutting tools used in machine tools such as lathes, milling machines, multiple drill presses, and the like. They are made from extremely hard and durable metal alloys capable of withstanding considerable abrasion and heat. Most of them are tipped with carbide, and some of them are diamond-tipped for ultimate hardness. PCTs cost from $200 to $500 per pound, which makes them a prime candidate for consideration as a space-produced alloy material. Generally, the harder the PCT, the greater the cost. A PCT made of a very hard and durable alloy that could be made in the weightlessness of space where unusual metals could be mixed would have a market at a competitive price, especially if the space alloy PCT had a longer life or could be used at a faster cutting speed. Either of these two characteristics would make space alloy PCTs very desirable because machine down-time and lost production costs are very expensive. This is particularly true in factories where an increasing number of completely automatic, numerically controlled machine tools are being used.

We don't know if a good PCT alloy could be made in space, but every principle of metallurgy points in the right direction. That means that PCT alloys are going to be early candidates for *SpaceLab* research. This is supported by the fact that the market for PCTs is big.

In 1976, the total PCT market was a little over a billion dollars. By 1985 when space-made PCTs might be expected to penetrate the market, this will have grown to a forecast $2.6 billion market. By 2000, this may grow to $5.6 billion. Carbide-tipped PCTs presently account for about 50% of this market.

Any space-made alloy that could offer even the slightest improvement in PCT hardness, lifetime, or cutting speed could certainly be expected to capture at least 5% of the total market within 20 years, especially since some very exotic titanium and beryllium alloys are now being machined with great difficulty for high-temperature applications. Even if only 5% of the PCT market is held by space-made PCT alloys in 2000, this amounts to annual sales of $280 million. If

we find a really good PCT alloy that can be made in
orbit and can manage to capture 50% of the PCT market by the year 2000, that's $2.8 billion.

We've spoken thus far only of prosaic everyday industrial applications of space-made materials and
products, but there is one particular consumer product that promises to become one of the first—if not *the*
first—space product to be profitable in the 1980 decade: space jewelry.

This is no laughing matter because every trade route
in Europe and Asia became established to fulfill a market desire for a luxury—silk, myrrh, ambergris, am-
ber, and gems. Great cities stand at the ancient cross-
roads of these trade routes today, even though the
products that went through their ancient gates are no
longer in demand or are shipped by other means that
bypass the well-trodden trade routes. Without these
trade routes and the desire for luxuries, cities such as
Berlin, Prague, Paris, Wien, Warsaw, Moscow, Kiev,
Teheran, Baghdad, Jerusalem, Tashkent, Bombay,
Calcutta, and Hong Kong would be mere villages in-
distinguishable from millions of others. Luxury trade
has made wealthy those who survived, and destroyed
those who were not smart, shrewd, and brave. Wars
have been fought because of luxuries.

Jewelry is a natural initial space product. Precious
metals and gems that are made into jewelry retain
their value because of their glamor. They are always
marketable and their value actually increases with
time.

A space jewel does not have to possess unique physical properties. It does not have to be pretty. It must
only be (a) rare and (b) unavailable from Earth manufacture. It must be capable of being made only in the

weightlessness of space. It must also be readily identified.

The glamor and uniqueness of a piece of jewelry made from a space alloy could capture anywhere from 1% to 10% of the current jewelry market. In 1976, this total jewelry market amounted to $1.72 billion. By 1985, it will have grown to about $3.47 billion dollars and, by the year 2000, up to $5.22 billion. Even a mere 1% of this market is not pocket change—almost $35 million in 1985 alone!

Space jewelry stands the chance of being one of the very first profitable space products and one that is certain to be attempted.

When was the last time you had a cavity in a tooth plugged? You can look forward to that filling lasting about 20 years. The filling material is an alloy called an amalgam, usually a mixture of mercury and silver that solidifies and crystallizes at room temperature. Dentists and dental patients would dearly love to have a better filling material. Current filling amalgams have both a higher heat transmission factor than tooth material and a different coefficient of thermal expansion. A thermo–setting fiber-reinforced noble metal polymer made in space (nobody has managed to make such a thing here yet) could find a market among the 150,000 dentists in the United States.

As this is being written, a tremendous amount of preliminary research work is going into the possibility of making new, improved, and high-purity biologicals and pharmaceuticals in space. It is known that a number of large pharmaceutical manufacturers are working in confidence with NASA at George C. Marshall Space Flight Center in Huntsville, Alabama. McDonnell-Douglas Corporation in St. Louis, Missouri

has compiled several reports for NASA Marshall
Space Flight Center on the subject of pharmaceuti-
cals. These reports are not government classified, but
I could get copies *only* if I agreed in writing not to dis-
cuss any of the contents. Since I was writing this book,
I could not agree to this gag rule.

The content of these pharmaceutical reports is ap-
parently so important, gives such an overwhelming
competitive advantage, and is so potentially profitable that the drug companies who participated and
are now participating do not want to give away any
information whatsoever. This is understandable in
an industry as highly competitive as pharmaceuticals. It is therefore obvious that improved drugs,
biologicals, and pharmaceuticals will be coming
from space processing operations in the 1980 time
period. Billions of dollars will be involved in research, production, and sales.

What makes the space environment so unique and
important for the production of pharmaceuticals and
biologicals? First of all, the absence of gravity makes
cell surface charge the dominant force, making possible new and non-destructive methods of cell separation. For example, blood components are quite sus-
ceptible to physical damage from Earthly separation
methods. In the weightlessness of orbit, we can em-
ploy such techniques as electrophoresis, a method
that uses electric fields to separate different complex
molecules. Electrophoresis cannot be used on a large
scale on Earth because the slight heating effects of the
electric field cause convection within the fluid being
separated, thus causing contamination and even destruction of delicate biological materials. When the
influence of gravity is eliminated, conviction is no longer a problem; heated material doesn't rise in zero–g.

Space pharmaceutical operations using various techniques could do an outstanding job of separating such materials as urokinase, pancreatic cells, pituitary cells, lymphocytes, granulocytes, macrophages, bone marrow, and sperm cells—all difficult to obtain on Earth. The ability to produce very pure materials in the weightlessness of space will certainly lead to vaccines of greater purity. Researchers in *SpaceLab* may even find a vaccine for cancer or even the legendary cure for the common cold.

But nobody is talking about the details of pharmaceutical processing techniques under study. Quite rightly, NASA is working with customers who wish to retain complete proprietary rights and to maintain the utmost secrecy until they have a product ready for the market. My own personal experience in attempting to gather the information points strongly to the fact that the potential here is considered high enough and good enough to warrant the utmost industrial secrecy.

The NASA Space Industrialization Study conducted by Science Applications, Inc. in 1977-1978 looked at a total of 147 different potential space products and materials . . . then time and money ran out because the funding for the study amounted to only one and a half man–years of effort. Only ten of these products/materials could be studied with any depth, but the total market for space materials/products by the turn of the century ranged from $1 billion to $10 billion per year for these ten examples alone.

There are going to be more than ten products and materials made in space by 1990. By the year 2000, there will be hundreds. We have yet to find out really what we can do out there in weightlessness. One thing is certain: we obviously do not know everything there is to know about the behavior of industrial processes in the absence of gravity, and a whole generation or more of space industrial engineers will have an exciting time finding out.

And somebody is going to make a very large amount of money, even though the risk is very high right now. This has always been the case in free societies throughout history. Yes, there will be spectacular failures as well. While it is true that hundreds of horses run races and only a few win, you cannot win on a horse race unless you make that bet in the first place. One horse is always faster than the rest; *but which one?*

A reminder: we are not talking about all this happening at some indeterminate future date. We are talking about the strong possibility of it happening within the next 10 to 12 years. Even if there are delays caused by politics or wars, the time only stretches out to 20 years. Most of you reading this will be using a space-made product in your lifetime; some of you will be making these products in space; and a few of you will be very rich because you bet on the right horse, risked your life savings, and worked like hell to make it happen.

Everything discussed here can happen in the 1980 decade because all the space technology necessary to make them happen is either already in place or will be ready to use during the coming decade. The NASA Space Shuttle will be available and capable of carrying payloads up to 65,000 pounds into Earth orbit; although the Shuttle has nagging little problems, these are engineering problems that accompany any new design that pushes the very limits of the current state of the art. These problems and the other ones that will inevitably crop up during the first few development flights can be solved and will be solved. Space Shuttle will work. So will *SpaceLab*, giving us the opportunity to study many of the things we touched upon in this chapter. The Small Self Contained Payload program, the Getaway Specials, will turn out to be one of the very best ideas NASA has ever had for involving the public in space activities, and there will be some spectacular successes that come from the Getaway Specials.

Two different unmanned upper-stages to be carried aloft in the Shuttle payload bay will be available for putting satellites into the higher geosynchronous orbit. Such upper states are now being developed both under government contract and by private enterprise. Thus, we will have the capability to do some of the things with communications satellites that we discussed previously, and use this capability for space manufacturing, too.

An additional power supply for the Shuttle is under development, the so-called "25 Kilowatt Power Module" that will greatly increase the electrical power available to experimenters on the Shuttle orbiter. The power module will be a solar-powered unit that will fold up to fit into the Shuttle payload bay with room left over for *SpaceLab* and other experimental payloads.

In the 1980 decade, we will also see the development and deployment of "free-flying" power modules. The obvious first step in this direction is to make *SpaceLab* self-sufficient apart from the Shuttle orbiter, take it into orbit with the Shuttle, and leave it there for 30 days or more, thus freeing up a Shuttle orbiter for other tasks. This will lead to two types of free–flying modules: the unmanned type with completely automated space processing activities, and the manned

type (such as the Soviet *Salyut*) where space processing activity involves people and the Shuttle brings up
a new factory shift every few weeks.

Eventually, there will be several of these grouped
together in one orbital location because it will be easier and more economical for a single Space Shuttle
Orbiter to bring up a new crew and new supplies for
several of these units on one flight.

Plans for utilizing the huge external tank of the Shuttle are also being considered. The normal mission plan
currently calls for the external tank to be dropped off
when the orbiter is only a few hundred feet-per-second
shy of orbital velocity. Empty of fuel, the tank would
drop back into the Indian Ocean and be destroyed; it's
only a cheap aluminum tank with some pipes on it.
However, the fuel tank is a pressure vessel and, as
such, will be useful in orbit. It's also big: 154 feet long
and 27.5 feet in diameter, with an internal volume of
nearly 70,000 cubic feet. That is several times the volume available in *Skylab*. In fact, it is more than equivalent to a factory with eight-foot-high ceilings and a
floor space of more than 8600 square feet—"more" because in weightlessness you can use nearly every cubic
foot of that huge volume. It's insulated with more than
an inch of foam plastic and it will hold more than one
atmosphere of pressure.

By off-loading a small proportion of payload or by
adding strap-on solid propellant boosters, it is possible to put this huge external fuel tank in orbit where it
can be used as the basis for a "space industrial park,"
an early space station that can be had almost for free.

Thus, everything is there. We're just going to have
to do it. By 1990, there can be hundreds of renovated
Shuttle fuel tanks in near-Earth orbit, linked together
as space industrial parks and festooned with the blue

In the 1980s, the first space laboratories and space factories could be installed in Space Shuttle External Tanks (ET) that are placed in orbit by the Shuttle at a slight cost in terms of payload capability. Once in orbit and equipped with the 25-kilowatt power module being developed for Shuttle use, the ET "space station" could serve as a nucleus for many space operations, both scientific and commercial.

solar panels of power supply modules and glowing red expanses of heat radiators. There may be as many as several hundred people living in space for periods up to several months, as two Soviet cosmonauts are doing even as I write this. There will be free-flying modules making things of value for Earth below. And the second phase of the space enterprise, *products*, will be well under way.

CHAPTER FIVE

"The world is running out of energy. All of us are going to have to cut back our use of energy and all of us are going to have to sacrifice. We're very wasteful, and this sacrifice will be good for us!"

Like hell! Sacrificing means giving up. The American people won't do it as long as there is an alternative that they can work on to improve the situation and to solve the problem. Anybody who tells you that you must sacrifice really means that you've got to give up something so that he can have a little more and so that he can tell you what to do with what little you've got left.

I have a big surprise for you: We are not running out of energy. There is no honest forecast of the future that shows energy demand exceeding energy supplies for the next 50 years, at any rate. The crystal ball gets very cloudy beyond that point.

Back in 1976, when NASA asked Dr. J. Peter Vajk, Dr. Ralph Sklarew, Gerald W. Driggers, Paul L. Siegler, Robert Salkeld, and myself to take a close look at space industrialization, we all initially felt that the "limits to growth" would act as a "driver" to "push" us into space industrialization. It was the simplest and easiest possible rationale to justify the industrialization of space. So we went looking for data to confirm this conjecture.

Much to our surprise and dismay (because we then had to come up with a different rationale), we discovered that, out to the year 2025, there was no "excess of demand over supply" of coal, petroleum, natural gas, uranium, iron, aluminum, chromium, cobalt, columbium, copper, lead, manganese, mercury, nickel, the platinum group metals, tin, titanium, tungsten, vanadium, zinc, fluorine, phosphates, corn, rice, wheat, cattle, pigs, or sheep. To quote the lengthy report based on the very latest data compiled by experts at Science Applications, Inc., "The spectre of impending scarcities does not, therefore, provide a credible basis for the political support necessary to mount a major thrust into space at public expense on a crash program schedule. The economic value of energy and minerals imported from space may be significant and may provide sufficient motivations for space industrialization; these possibilities should not be dismissed lightly. But their justification during the period of interest of this study must be found elsewhere. 'Limits to growth' cannot justify space industrialization during the next three or more decades."

This means (if the data is true) that any time somebody tells you that there is a "shortage" in the next quarter of a century, you will know that the shortage is very probably political in nature. So question it carefully and suspect the motives of those who cry "shortage" and "sacrifice."

That's great news, but where does that leave us at the gasoline pumps or when the utility bill comes in at the end of each month? Where does that leave us when environmental controls will not permit the mining of coal for power plants? When somebody finally wises up to the fact that coal-fired power plants put more radioactivity into the atmosphere in the form of Carbon-14 than ever leaked out of Three Mile Island? When hysteria and politics, acting in ignorance of nuclear technology, force the closure of nuclear power plants or prohibit building new ones?

I am personally opposed to the continued use of coal, natural gas, and petroleum as energy sources for an indefinite time into the future. But not for the reasons you might suspect. Coal, natural gas, and petroleum are all exceedingly valuable chemical feedstocks that form the basis for the manufacture of plastics, adhesives, rubber, synthetic fabrics, electrical insulation, and pharmaceuticals, among other things. Take away coal, natural gas, and crude oil; your world will immediately collapse around you. If you do not believe this, pause to look at things around you and ask yourself how many of them are made from (or with the assistance of) modern industrial chemistry whose feedstocks come from coal, natural gas, and crude oil.

Granted: There is no immediate shortage of energy sources among the fossil fuels of planet Earth. Granted: These fossil fuels will someday run out, but most probably not within the next 50 years. Granted: We should not use them as energy sources but as chemical feedstocks.

Where, then, do we get the energy that we need to glue our social organization together?

Nuclear fission? Well, we're going to run out of available uranium, too. Nuclear fission power isn't safe; Three Mile Island proved that. But it is *safer* than any other energy source we currently have. Let's use it only as a bridge to something better and accept the risk for less than a century only because we must.

Nuclear fusion? Yes, but who knows how to build

and operate and extract energy from nuclear fusion right now? We can build thermonuclear bombs, but trying to harness the energy of one of those is like trying to harness the electricity of a lightning bolt. They're both very sudden stuff.

Geothermal? Yes, because the interior of the Earth is pretty hot and will remain hot for a long time yet to come. We now have the technology to drill very deep holes to tap the heat of Earth's interior; we got that technology from learning how to drill very deep off-shore oil wells while the environmentalists were pa-rading back and forth along the beaches, demanding that it be stopped. Geothermal energy will be cheap, available, and environmentally acceptable. We'll use it.

Hydropower? Yes, we'll use that, too, because you never want to put all your eggs in one basket. Yes, the building of dams and their attendant reservoirs will screw up a couple hundred square miles of the envi-ronment. Or will it? Sure, a new lake is hell on the land animals who lived there, but it's pretty neat for the fish who swim and the water flora that develop in the new lake. We have built a lot of hydroelectric dams in the past hundred years, and I agree that we have changed the local environment as a result; but I can-not agree that we have screwed it up. Just changed it. (In the Phoenix, Arizona area, environmentalists pre-vented the building of a needed dam because it would disrupt the nests of five bald eagles. In the resulting floods, the hydropower went to waste, several people were killed, thousands were left homeless, millions of dollars of property and personal possessions were de-stroyed . . . and the flood wiped out the bald eagles and their nests in the process.)

But there is one energy source upon which everything on Earth has always depended: a natural hydro-gen-helium fusion reactor called the Sun.

Solar energy has been a neglected technology in the past because other forms of energy were cheaper and their technologies were mature. Solar energy is, how-ever, the energy source of the future. It suffers from two serious drawbacks when you try to harness it on the Earth's surface: (a) the Sun doesn't shine on any given geographical location constantly, and when you need it most it isn't there—when it's cloudy, in the winter and at night; and (b) although the Sun puts into the Earth's environment every hour 4285 times as much energy as the human race produces by the burn-ing of wood, coal, natural gas, and crude oil, it isn't very concentrated—only three-tenths of a calorie per square inch per minute. Thin stuff.

What we really need to do in order to harness solar energy, therefore, is to convert it to electricity so that we can easily and cheaply transport it where we want it. We must put our solar electric power plant in a lo-cation where the Sun shines all the time and where we can build very, very large structures to collect the dif-fuse solar energy.

The place to do this is in space.

But we must then answer several questions.

How do we do it in space and get the electricity back to the surface of the Earth?

Several methods have been proposed.

Dr. Krafft A. Ehricke has suggested the "soletta" or "little sun" approach. A soletta is a collection of orbit-ing mirrors that will reflect sunlight back to Earth. A soletta in geosynchronous orbit would be able to pro-vide a constant source of solar energy to units at a given location on the Earth, day or night, except dur-ing cloudy weather. Solar energy falling directly on a solar power plant on Earth during daylight could be supplemented by the reflected energy from the soletta in space. Photovoltaic units (solar cells) on the ground could be used to convert this solar energy directly to electricity. Or the solar energy could be used to heat water to steam and thus operate turboelectric generators. All of this involves technology that we understand and can handle, but it suffers from a number of drawbacks.

First of all, a soletta will have to be very large in order to reflect enough solar energy to make it worthwhile. In order to reflect about 75% of the equivalent noon-time solar energy back to Earth, a soletta will range in size from about 200 square miles to 2500 square miles in area. Thus, a large soletta would be larger than the State of Delaware or about twice the size of the State of Rhode Island. There is no problem in building this large a structure in space, except that we haven't done it yet (but we will). To take advantage of weightlessness, such structures can be fabricated in orbit, preferably from composite epoxy materials at first. Later on, we'll see how such a large structure in space can be put together. The reflecting units of the soletta can be thin films of plastic such as mylar or kevlar that are given a thin coating of silver or aluminum in space.

A second problem involves the fact that a soletta won't work all the time except in parts of the world where there are few cloudy days.

But the major problem appears to be ecological. We don't know what effect a constant beam of solar energy might have upon both weather and climate—climate being the long-term trends of weather patterns. A small sun in the sky constantly will most certainly have its effects upon life forms in the receiving area on Earth.

A smaller version of the soletta called the "lunetta" would certainly find uses for nighttime illumination without some of the possible ecological effects. Lunettas, being smaller, would be easier and cheaper to build. It would be a good guess that a few lunettas might be tried out first to check both the space construction side of the picture and the terrestrial effects as well.

The prime candidate for space energy at the moment appears to be the Solar Power Satellite (SPS) or Sunsat, a concept that originated with Dr. Peter E. Glaser of Arthur D. Little, Inc. in 1968.

An SPS would be a very large array of photovoltaic cells about 25 square miles in area—about 8 miles long and 3 miles wide. The electricity generated by this solar cell array would be converted to microwaves with a frequency of approximately 2450 megaHertz. These microwaves would be beamed from the SPS in geosynchronous orbit down to a large rectifying antenna or "rectenna" on the Earth's surface. This rectenna would cover an area of about 10 miles by 15 miles and be made up of elements looking much like aluminum roofs set 10 to 12 feet above the ground. The rectenna itself is very simple, cheap, and easy to build and maintain. It can be built with relatively unskilled labor, an important point to keep in mind when we discuss the international aspects later. The rectenna would convert the microwave energy to the sort of voltages and frequencies that would match the local electric utility network, and the electricity thus picked up from the SPS would be available on the existing electric power grid. Or, for various international customers, it can be used for other purposes as we will later see.

The SPS is in nearly constant sunlight, being eclipsed by the Earth's shadow only briefly for an hour or so every few months. The weather over the rectenna can be clear or cloudy because the microwave beam will penetrate clouds. The losses due to the passage of the microwave beam through the Earth's atmosphere are but a fraction of a percent and it is highly doubtful if they will have any environmental effect upon the atmosphere, weather, or climate. Tests have already been conducted at the big radio telescope at Aricebo, Puerto Rico, to determine the effects of an SPS microwave beam on the ionosphere, the Earth's upper atmosphere. No effects were detected.

There has been some concern voiced about the biological effects of the microwave beam. Would it harm a bird that flew through the beam over the rectenna? Would it harm an animal grazing under the rectenna elements? What would the microwave energy do to human beings?

At the center of the microwave beam, the energy density would be only about 23 milliwatts per square centimeter. Frankly, we do not know at this time whether microwave energy of this density would harm a bird flying over the rectenna.

At the edge of the rectenna on the fringe of the microwave beam, the energy density would be about one milliwatt per square centimeter, which is well below the levels that are known to cause biological damage such as cataracts, heart disease, blood changes, or genetic damage.

However, I should point out that nothing about the SPS design is yet "frozen in concrete." If it turns out that the microwave beam could be dangerous to life

Solar power satellites (SPS) in geosynchronous Earth orbit utilize huge photovoltaic solar energy collectors. The electricity generated by the constant and abundant sunlight of space is then beamed to the Earth's surface on a radio beam.

forms in its center, it is possible to design the system to use a more diffuse beam with an energy density far below that which causes any biological damage. We would just make the rectenna bigger.

If it turns out that microwave beaming is unacceptable for any of a number of reasons, technical or political, other methods of power beaming have been suggested. J. Frank Coneybear of Ball Brothers Research has studied the possibility of beaming the energy to Earth via diffuse, defocused laser beams. Such a beaming method could make use of infra-red lasers operating at a frequency in one of the "windows" of the atmosphere where moisture such as clouds and fog would not interact with the beam. Also, such a laser beam is not a destructive sort of weapon out of *Star Wars*. It is unfortunate that the laser carries the stigma of a weapon because lasers are being used every day for very peaceful and useful industrial purposes.

And if either microwave beams or laser beams turn out to be unsuitable for sending the electrical energy of an SPS back to Earth, there may be other approaches to the problem.

Be that as it may, let's ask the inevitable question: Can an SPS do much of anything to alleviate the energy situation here on Earth? The answer is "yes."

The "baseline" size for an economical SPS of the physical dimensions mentioned above (and the "baseline" SPS currently under study by the U.S. Department of Energy with the assistance of NASA) would generate 5,000,000,000 watts of electrical power—five gigawatts. A far better SPS in terms of economy would be a 10–gigawatt unit.

The United States' total electric power capacity in 1975 was 228,000,000,000 watts (228,000,000 kilowatts). By the year 2000, assuming a constant 35% annual growth rate based upon historic trends going

back to 1925, the U.S. capacity should have risen to
940,000,000,000 watts (940,000,000 kilowatts). This is
a 412% increase, which means a lot more coal-fired
and nuclear electric generating plants . . . unless we
get an SPS system on-line starting in 1990.

Here's the way it looks, assuming a single SPS is designed for 10 gigawatts (10,000,000,000 watts):

Year	New SPS on-line	Total SPS on-line
1990	1	1
1995	9	10
2000	14	24
2005	32	56
2010	43	99
2015	59	158
2020	79	237
2025	107	344

Can we do it at all? Yes, providing. . . .

Right now, we need to begin proving out the whole
SPS concept. Several studies have been conducted already, including one for the Department of Energy
that resulted in a stack of white papers on a variety of
subjects ranging from public acceptance to financial
and management systems. There were two big question marks that appeared all the way through all of
these white papers: (a) could it be done technically?
and (b) could it be done economically?

We need to find the answers to these questions in the
1980 decade if the 1990 decade is to be the decade of
space power. I believe the answers to these two questions will come out on the positive side. I also believe
that the answers to these questions cannot and will
not be determined by more studies; we've reached the
point with SPS where we've got to go build some hardware and get hard answers.

The Space Shuttle will permit us to take the first steps. We need to know several things first: (a) can we build large structures in space as some early work indicates that we can? (b) what system is actually the best—photovoltaic, turboelectric, microwave beaming, laser beaming, something else? and (c) what system is most economical, what are the actual costs, and how do we go about actually building the SPS system that we finally decide upon?

We will be able to answer these questions in the 1980 decade using the Space Shuttle. It will involve a step-by step program with definite milestones of the go/no-go type. We must first get some prototype SPS hardware into space in the Shuttle and try it out. We must develop the capability to fabricate very large structures in space. We must check out the ecological and biological effects of both microwave and laser power beaming. We must build a small rectenna on the Earth's surface, probably in the western United States, to check out rectenna design, environmental impact, and biological effects as well as the nit-picking details of engineering and technology. By the year 1987, we should have reached a milestone that will provide us with enough data to make a decision: Do we now build a pilot SPS in orbit?

A pilot plant is a commonplace industrial operation where you try out a new process or operation on a small scale, learning and modifying as you go, before you commit big bucks to full-sized plants. Some of the things you may have learned during the experimental and developmental phases when things were tested in isolation from one another may not work worth a hill of beans when you put them together as a system. Any engineer will tell you that the early development work is a snap compared to the nit-picking, fiddling, fine-tuning, tweaking, and minor modifications that follow all the mathematics and designing and powering-up. Systems don't work perfectly at first. If they did, there would be no need for test pilots, there would be no product recalls, and engines wouldn't occasionally fall off airplanes. Nuclear power plants wouldn't occasionally have problems, and ordinary steam power plants wouldn't occasionally have a boiler explosion. A lot of engineering talent involves simply getting the damned system to work in the first place . . . and once you've got it working, let it the hell and gone alone.

A pilot SPS in orbit and ground-based rectenna operating between 1987 and 1989 would give us the sort of data we would need to evaluate the risks, establish the costs, and then decide whether or not to proceed with a complete SPS system. Because if the decision is to go, it begins to get expensive.

As SPS is going to weigh more than 50 million pounds. Every pound of that mass is, at first, going to have to be hauled up from the Earth's surface by rockets to low-Earth orbit, then boosted to geosynchronous orbit where it can be assembled into an SPS. Assemble the whole thing in a 200-mile-high Earth orbit and then boost it out to the 22,200-mile geosynchronous orbit, you say? Not a fragile solar array of 30 to 50 square miles! You build such a huge structure on site so that you don't have to move it . . . all you have to do is to twist it a little now and then and shove it gently occasionally to keep it lined up with the Sun and to maintain its orbital position. You do *not* try to accelerate it out of low orbit to geosynch, not unless you want to build it stronger and therefore heavier than need be.

We can't build the SPS system with the Space Shuttle. We must have a bigger and more extensive space transportation system to do it. We will need Heavy-Lift Launch Vehicles capable of lifting not a mere 65,000 pounds to low-Earth orbit, but millions of pounds at a time up to geosynch orbit. We will need personnel shuttles, inter-orbit tugs, inter-orbit transfer vehicles, on-orbit remote teleoperators, and habitats where people can live while they are building the SPS in geosynch. These construction crews will have to be rotated back to Earth from time to time. And the crews in space will need a storm cellar, an enclosure that they can duck into fast and that is protected against the radiation from a solar flare lest said solar flare snuff out their candles. (We can expect to lose some people building an SPS because it is an inevitable fact of life; every large construction job on Earth proceeds with a budgeted estimate of the number of human lives that are going to be lost during construction. It's not inhumane in the least, just realistic.)

By 1990, we could have the first 10-gigawatt SPS in geosynch orbit and pumping electrical power back to our electrical power grids on Earth.

Thereafter, we've got to keep building them for a few years to meet the increasing electric power requirements here on Earth.

But there's gotta be an end to this, right? How long can we keep on building SPS units if the demand for electric power increases by 35% every year? Sooner or later, we've ringed the Earth with SPS units!

You must keep in mind the engineer's approach to things. All systems are always working and always progressing together.

Right now, about 66% of the electrical power generated in the United States is consumed by industry with only about 33% being used for heating and lighting homes.

The 1980 decade will have seen the beginning of space processing as a profitable venture. During the 1990 decade, more and more industry will be moved into space for a number of reasons. First, it will be a better place for industrial operations. Secondly, space industry doesn't pollute the Earth's biosphere. Third, because of the build-up of the space transportation system in the 1990s to bring the SPS system on-line, space transportation costs could fall as low as $10 per pound.

By the first decade of the 21st Century, an interesting thing happens: we begin to greatly decrease the cost of building SPS units by utilizing extraterrestrial materials! More about this later, but we cannot forever go on hauling thousands and thousands of tons of material up through Earth's strong gravity well. Once we have a basic space transportation system in place, it will be easier and cheaper to go to the planetoid belt between Mars and Jupiter where there is no gravity well except the rather diffuse one of the Sun to contend with. And we will return to the Moon for raw materials that we already know are there in quantity—aluminum, silicon, and titanium, among others.

Our early studies and conversations with existing electrical utility companies indicate that it is going to be possible to build a single 10-gigawatt SPS unit for about the cost of an equivalent coal-fired Earth-based power plant—a cost ranging from $1500 to $2000 per kilowatt-installed. As we convert from using terrestrial materials to extraterrestrial materials, the costs drop by more than 50%.

Thus, the big SPS units built in the 2000–2010 decade are going to cost less than the ones built in the 1990–1995 time period.

And we will begin to use this space transportation

capability to supply not only our space operations, but also to provide new space industries with the materials they need—industries such as the primary metals industry.

Slowly, during the first two to three decades of the 21st century heavy industry will begin to move off Earth because (a) energy is going to be cheaper and more available out there, (b) raw materials will be available out there, (c) transportation systems will be available to move raw materials around and to deliver finished products to markets on Earth and in space, and (d) there will be no problem with stiff and restrictive environmental protection laws in space!

This means that the industrial electric power load of Earth and particularly the United States and other industrialized, high–tech countries on Earth, is going to be reduced in some cases by as much as 50% to 60%.

At that point, we begin to shut down and dismantle the old nuclear power plants and the old coal-fired and oil-fired power plants. We don't need them any more once we have 200 to 250 SPS units in orbit supplying electric power to us. What excess we may need beyond that we can obtain from geothermal and hydroelectric sources.

Thus, space energy and Earth energy comprise an interlocked system. If we can technically and economically build an SPS system—and we will be able to find out within ten years if we can—we not only become able to supply our major electrical energy needs from space, but we get a few extras in the bargain. We get a space transportation system. This space transportation system reduces transportation costs to the point where it becomes both economical and feasible for industry to move into space in a bigger way. The space transportation system also permits us to begin to utilize the raw material resources of the Solar System that are out there waiting for us. As we therefore move more and more industry off Earth and into space, our electric power requirements decrease. As a result, we can shut down the nukes and bank the fires of the coal plants without worrying about freezing in the dark.

This is called "synergism," which doesn't mean that it's a sin to go into space. It *will* be a sin if we do not take this great opportunity to use space to help solve our problems; it *will* be a sin if we just sit here slipping into more and more inaction, "sacrifice," and shortages as we go further and further on the skids, eventually falling back into a New Dark Ages in the 21st Century.

"There is one great problem about slipping back into the New Dark Ages," warns Dr. Krafft A. Ehricke. "This time, our fingers are on the nuclear triggers."

This can happen very suddenly. Anthropologist Carleton S. Coon points out that "man has been converting energy into social structure; as he has drawn more and more energy from Earth's natural resources, he has organized himself into social organizations of increasing size and complexity."

If the energy crunch worsens and becomes a true shortage according to the "limits of growth" philosophy, the very first social organizations to fail will be the most recent and most complex ones: our international ones. This is more than the UN. It's NATO. It's SALT. It's all the international agreements, treaties, and compromises we have managed to put together over the years to keep most of us from killing some of the rest of us some of the time. Without our international organizations, supported by the increased energy demands of their structure, we could slip back more than 500 years in the blink of an eye. Our ancestors a mere 25 generations ago were barbarians and savages compared to us today. If you want to put nuclear and thermonuclear weapons in the hands of Timurlane, Napoleon, Atilla, Ghengis Khan, Adolph Hitler, and their ilk, all you have to do is shut down the nukes *right now*, close down the coal-fired plants because they pollute the atmosphere, and prevent the building of hydroelectric projects because they threaten fish, birds, or other animals; pretty soon there won't be any animals, fish, or birds because we will either have eaten them or destroyed them with fallout.

Mother Nature is telling us right now: "The energy you need is there. Find out how to use it or die."

Neat philosophical points, perhaps, but they don't cut much ice when it comes to convincing a bank, a government, or a corporation to build and operate an SPS system. We've just been talking about social costs, which may appeal only to a person's better nature. Robert Heinlein warns us never to do that because the person may not have a better nature; you can get more done by appealing to his personal interest instead.

Item to appeal to personal interest: The people who take the risks and provide the capital and build the SPS units and operate the system are going to make a great deal of money.

Yes, an SPS is expensive—about the same cost as a similar size coal-fired power plant here on Earth. At $2000 per kilowatt installed, the first one is going to cost you an estimated $20 billion. (Choke!) But it doesn't make any difference if you build an SPS or a coal-fired plant on Earth: it's going to cost you the same number of bucks per kilowatt. It doesn't make any difference whether you build your new electric power plants here or in space, it's going to cost you just about the same or perhaps more to do it on Earth. If you do it on Earth, you will be subject to environmental controls of increasing severity. Within 20 years or less, you will probably be fighting for coal allotments. You will be paying more and more for coal and oil.

Do it in space, and you are collecting a renewable energy resource that is already there, waiting to be used, not subject to allotment, and available for a long time yet to come. Do it in space and you will have minimal environmental impact, the worst being the possibility of cooking a bird that flies into a concentrated microwave beam; but birds get killed by the thousands every day on high-voltage electric transmission towers anyway. Do it in space and you will build an overall system that will move your biggest customers into space to follow you, where it will be cheaper to beam power to them.

What are the projected revenues? There are two sources today that can give us some inkling of the magnitude of the revenues that could be expected. Studies done by Dr. Gerard K. O'Neill and his associates at Princeton University indicate that SPS power could be made available at 7 mils per kilowatt hour at the interface between the rectenna and the electric power grid. Using more conservative figures, Dr. Peter E. Glaser and his associates at Arthur D. Little, Inc. have calculated an interface cost of 27 mils per kilowatt hour.

A single 10-gigawatt SPS could produce an annual revenue ranging from about $6 million to about $2.4 billion. From a 200-unit SPS system, this is an annual revenue ranging from $1.23 billion up to $480 billion.

Over an estimated 30-year SPS lifetime, a single unit could earn from about $190 million to about $71 billion. According to the Princeton figures, you couldn't get a return on investment at 7 mils per kilowatt-hour unless extraterrestrial materials are used. On the other hand, a single SPS unit can make as much as $51 billion total over a 30-year life at 27 mils per kilowatt hour, using only terrestrial resources.

The true and accurate economics will lie somewhere between the two or, most probably, better than forecast if the switch to extraterrestrial materials for building an SPS can take place around the year 2000.

Answer to the question: Can you make money with space power? *Yes.* Lots of it. Provided all the factors to be experimented with and determined with great economic and technical accuracy in the 1980–1987 time period turn out to be favorable.

If any area of space industrialization provides the "push" to do it at all, space energy is that area. It can begin with equipment and technology we have in hand in the 1980 decade. It can begin to go on-line in the 1990 decade. By the year 2000, it can begin to provide a return on investment. And it has some beneficial consequences—a space transportation system, the capability to utilize ET materials, the assumption of the base energy load from Earth facilities, and the rationale for initiation of transfer of heavier industrial operations off the Earth to reduce the Earth-based energy load which will permit the retirement of some of the coal and nuke electric plants on Earth.

Energy? It's all around us, waiting to be utilized. There is no shortage if we get busy and do something about it . . . soon.

CHAPTER SIX

In discussing three of the elements of the space enterprise—communications, products, and energy—the development of a suitable space transportation system was considered as a *fait accompli*. Actually, we do not yet have a space transportation system but we are about to get one and probably will have it by the time you read these words.

At the moment (late 1979) the development of our first real space transportation system, the NASA Space Shuttle, is the pacing item of the space enterprise. Once we have it, things other than communications, navigation, information transfer, earth resources, and meteorological satellites can begin to happen.

After that, the decisions regarding how, when, and how fast to proceed with various aspects of the space enterprise will drive the space transportation systems and their developments.

We should define our terms right from the start and agree on what we mean by a "space transportation system."

A space transportation system is an integrated collection of space–traveling vehicles, ground facilities, and space facilities that will permit and allow the transfer of both people and cargo from Point A to Point B around the inner Solar System—from the orbit of Mercury out to the orbit of Jupiter—on a scheduled basis with a reasonable cost, a high reliability of completing the transfer, and an acceptable return on investment.

Space transportation should and must be viewed in the same light as a railroad, a shipping line, a truck line, or an airline: as a common carrier. If it is not operated on a profitable basis, somebody is going to have to subsidize it so that it can pay its bills. It must operate on a reliable basis or nobody is going to entrust people or valuable cargo to it. It must operate on a scheduled basis so that customers will know when to ship or travel and when to expect arrival.

A space transportation system is *not* just a spaceship. It is *not* a Space Shuttle. It is *not* a single–stage–to–orbit spaceship. It is *not* a space tug. It is *all* of these things, *plus*: the supporting system that provides fuel for the vehicles where and when needed; the repair and refurbishment facilities that keep the ships operating when something goes wrong or when a regular inspection is required, and the facility for handling both people and cargo here on Earth, in space, and on other celestial bodies of the inner Solar System.

Now we are about to start using the first rudimentary part of a space transportation system, the NASA Space Shuttle. We have never really had a space transportation system before. We have had a series of expendable devices that operated at great cost on irregular schedules with a questionable reliability.

The NASA Space Shuttle will provide several of the requirements of a space transportation system. It will be able to transfer up to 65,000 pounds of cargo and up to seven people at a time to near-Earth orbit and return. It will be able to do this on a regularly-scheduled basis. But it will not be able to do it at a reasonable cost and with a reasonable return on investment.

This is because the NASA Space Shuttle wasn't designed and built to become the transportation system of the space enterprise. The whole concept of the space enterprise and the Third Industrial Revolution came along after the Shuttle was conceived, the design frozen and the first metal cut. Space Shuttle was the last surviving remnant of the NASA Manned Mars Mission whose planning goal was to put a manned expedition on Mars in the 1990 decade. This was laid out in the halcyon days of the 1960s when it looked like the bubbling spring of tax waters would never dry up. When the news media grew weary of space and convinced the Congress that America had other, more immediate priorities, and while the war in southeast Asia was sopping up our wealth and resources and manpower, Congress began chopping the space program budget. After all, when you've seen one Moon landing, you've seen them all . . . One by one, the elements of the manned Mars mission were dropped until only one remained: the manned, reusable Space Shuttle with the capability of putting 65,000 pounds into orbit and returning to be used again. The payload size and weight was actually determined by the requirement of the Mars mission. Later plans for a big space station were also cut, leaving the Space Shuttle all alone and looking for a job.

Ten years later, the Space Shuttle becomes reality, the last survivor of a grand dream and the hope of the space enterprise. Thanks to the 65,000–pound payload, we can really think about doing something useful in space!

It isn't cheap. However, it's more economical than expendable converted military ballistic rockets. Even the huge Saturn-V had a cost of $500 per pound to low Earth orbit and was considered to be very efficient. That cost was an order of magnitude less than the first Earth satellites—*Explorer* and *Vanguard*—which ran about $5000 per pound. Orbiting a payload in the Space Shuttle will run about $325 per pound for a full dedicated 65,000-pound payload. A Getaway Special flown on a space-available payload-of-opportunity basis will cost about $50 per pound.

This is still too much money for space transportation, and we will have to develop new and more efficient vehicles to bring these costs down. After all, we must keep always in mind the fact that the NASA Space Shuttle is really a far-out pioneering effort that is stretching the state of the art to its very limit and trying to do things that have not been done before.

Never before has there been a conscious attempt to design and build a space vehicle that can be used repeatedly for as much as a hundred flights. Until now, a space vehicle was designed for only a single flight, to be thrown away or, if recovered, to be retired to the National Air and Space Museum.

The Space Shuttle meant applying airliner design philosophy to a rocket vehicle, and it wasn't an easy accomplishment. The design of a very high performance liquid rocket engine that could be throttled, stopped, started, and operated for thousands of seconds sounds commonplace to those of us who are accustomed to driving automobiles that are expected to last for at least 50,000 miles (or about 1500 working hours). But it wasn't an easy task for rocket engineers to accomplish because most rocket engines before the Space Shuttle had to operate for only a matter of a few

minutes . . . period. How do you go about designing a
thermal protection system to keep the Shuttle from
burning up when it enters the Earth's atmosphere at
more than 17 miles per second . . . for a hundred
flights? All previous space vehicles had to do that trick
once and only once.

So the NASA Space Shuttle is a real breakthrough,
and don't forget it. It is critical that it works and works
right. And it will. There have been and will continue
to be little engineering bugs that show up during operations, but this is true of any new automobile or airplane design as well. The big, juicy problems that will
be gleefully reported by the news media are only the
sort of debugging process that any new device goes
through. When you read about them, remember all the
time and effort it took to get the little annoying bugs
out of the last car you bought!

But we are going to have only five Space Shuttle Orbiters, six at the very most. Count on the fact that at
least one of these is going to be bent and therefore
written off at some point during the 1980 decade. And
the Space Shuttle Orbiters are going to wear out, just
like airplanes and cars do. Each Orbiter is designed
for a hundred flights; the engineers may and probably
will figure out a way to stretch the Orbiter lifetimes to
perhaps 150 flights, maybe 200 flights. But the NASA
Space Shuttle is going to become rapidly obsolete for
a number of reasons.

First of all, the Space Shuttle is going to teach us
how to do the Earth-to-orbit and return job cheaper
and easier:

Secondly, the Space Shuttle is going to create a real
need for increased traffic to orbit just because of all
the profitable things that are going to be discovered in
SpaceLab and all the wonderful new things that engi-

neers will discover that they can do with the "complexity inversion" that we discussed earlier. Five or six Space Shuttle Orbiters are not going to be able to handle the traffic requirements in the latter half of the 1980 decade. So new ones will have to be built. And the new ones will be different, cheaper, and more efficient.

Third, we cannot possibly construct a Solar Power Satellite system with just the Space Shuttle. True, we will use the Space Shuttle to get things started in that area, perhaps utilizing the Shuttle until 1987 for the pilot plant SPS. But beyond that point, the requirements to lift very large payloads to orbit on a more frequent basis simply outstrips the capabilities of the Space Shuttle.

We will need a Heavy–Lift Launch Vehicle, an HLLV.

And we can make one on an interim basis using Space Shuttle components—the solid rocket boosters, the ET, and a 150,000–pound cargo cannister with Space Shuttle engines strapped on its tail end. Cheap, quick, and dirty.

But to make Earth-to-orbit transportation cheaper, we are going to have to consider a completely reusable Earth-to-orbit vehicle by 1987-1990—a single-stage-to-orbit (SSTO) shuttle. Design studies on SSTO concepts have already started. Some of them use vertical takeoff and vertical landing (VTOVL); others use vertical takeoff and horizontal landing (VTOHL) like the NASA Space Shuttle. Others are designed around the advanced concept of horizontal takeoff and horizontal landing (HTOHL). This latter concept bears consideration, because it could take off from and land on an ordinary airport runway, requiring no special launching facilities. It is truly the airliner concept expanded into the space age.

But there will not be any single Space Shuttle follow–on Earth-to-orbit vehicle any more than there is only one type of airliner, or one type of ocean-going ship, or one type of railway car, or one kind of truck. The main requirement for Earth-to-orbit transportation in the late 1980s and 1990s is *reduced cost*. To reduce costs, you must specialize the vehicles. Thus, there will undoubtedly be at least two types of passenger-carrying shuttles: one sized for about 20-35 passengers, the other a larger passenger shuttle capable of carrying a hundred people or more. They will be the DC-3 and DC-10 of space, if you will. There will be several types of cargo-carrying ships. One may be totally expendable—a one-way launch vehicle that is never intended to return to Earth, its parts and components instead used for other vehicles and facilities in space. There will be a true Heavy–Lift Launch Vehicle, a single-stage-to-orbit monster capable of lofting a million pounds of payload or more to low-Earth orbit; it will be a reusable vehicle for the same reason that a 1200–foot, 700,000-ton oil supertanker is reusable. Boeing has come up with one such vehicle whose unusual shape earned it the apellation of "The Big Onion." There will be at least one type of smaller cargo vehicle with a payload-to-orbit of 20 tons or less; an express ship, if you will. If they need a new klystron on SPS-6, there is no need to dispatch a million-pound Big Onion to carry a couple hundred pounds to them on an emergency basis.

The objective of this Earth-to-orbit vehicle specialization is primarily to reduce costs. At $325 per pound, Shuttle is too expensive. When your Earth-made prod-

The "Big Onion" Heavy Lift–Launch Vehicle of 1989 punches its way up through the Earth's cloud deck with a payload of 400,000 pounds of SPS equipment. The HLLV is reusable and will return for a horizontal landing using its blunt aft end as an entry heat shield. Design is based on a Boeing study.

uct goes out the back door at about a dollar per pound complete, you can't even think of making it in space. It's too expensive when you've got to put 50 million pounds in orbit for each SPS you build; that's 769 NASA Space Shuttle flights to low-Earth orbit alone at $21 million per flight.

The first cost target should be and will be $25 per pound to low-Earth orbit. There is light at the end of the tunnel on this one: people like Robert Salkeld, who are deeply involved in advanced space transportation systems studies, can already foresee that we can achieve this goal by 1990 or before, using SSTO shuttles that can be built with technology in hand. This figure of $25 per pound puts the Boeing Big Onion total flight costs in the same league with the NASA Space Shuttle that carries far less payload.

The next big cost goal is $10 per pound to orbit. This is going to stretch the state of the art. We probably won't be able to achieve it until the 1990 decade. It will require real sophistication in spacecraft design, construction, and operation. It may mean that our Earth-launch vehicles will have to become even more specialized than indicated above. It may require such advanced concepts as actually "flying into space," a horizontal takeoff and a gradual climb at just under Mach-1 until you reach orbital velocity and orbital altitude. Since the speed of sound increases with altitude, this means that the flying-into-orbit ship continues to gain velocity as it climbs. It can use rocket engines of lower thrust because it isn't climbing vertically all the way; it is using the Earth's own atmosphere to provide lift and its propulsion to provide the excess of energy required to climb over that required to sustain level flight. It is rather surprising how fast you can "fly into orbit" with this concept. It's a lot easier on passengers because the acceleration remains low. It means that you can use reasonably straightforward aluminum aircraft construction and well-understood techniques of thermal protection. Such a ship doesn't get very hot, but it gets hot for a longer period of time than a conventional vertical rocket or the streamlined anvils of such historic spacecraft as the *Apollo*.

The cost-per-pound to orbit and the traffic demand are intimately interlinked in a positive feedback system. The moment the cost drops, the traffic model grows.

There are some things that you should do to maintain some perspective on the space transportation matter. First of all, go out on the observation deck and look around you the next time you are at Chicago's O'Hare International Airport, Denver's Stapleton International, Los Angeles International, Washington National, or JFK. Count the number of jet airliners that you can see, and multiply the number of jet airliners by $10 million; that will average things out to give you a rough estimate of the capital investment sitting there *on the ground*. There are just as many expensive airplanes in the air that you cannot see. Then remember that you are looking at only *one airport* out of some 300 major airports served by commercial jet airliners in the United States. Look around you at the airport, at the buildings, at the trucks and other ground vehicles that swarm around the jets or just sit waiting for another jet to land. Think of the kitchens that are preparing thousands of meals. Think of the massive investment in fueling facilities. Think of the thousands of people handling reservations, check-in, baggage handling, and even running the vacuum cleaners in the cabins of airliners waiting to receive

A horizontal takeoff, horizontal landing space shuttle of the 1990 decade trims orbit with its thrusters. Such a vehicle would not be much larger than the 1980 NASA Space Shuttle, but would be capable of single-stage-to-orbit operations and would be completely reusable, lowering space transportation costs below $25 per pound.

their next load of passengers. Think of the fact that an airline tries to keep one of those expensive jet airliners flying at least 10 hours per day, more if they can manage it, because it isn't making any money when it's sitting on the ground.

Now, put yourself in Orville Wright's shoes. Think of what he would have said if you had tried to tell him about this on that cold December morning at Kitty Hawk in 1903. Better yet, try to explain it to a banker in 1925. Consider what the reaction would have been in 1945 if you had tried to tell any airline president that within 20 years he would be gladly paying five times as much per airplane, that he would be using ten times as much fuel in these airplanes, and that his passenger traffic would go up by a factor of ten; tell him that to do this meant that every major airport in the world would have to be rebuilt with runways two miles long, that entirely new systems of air traffic control costing billions of dollars would be required, and that in spite of this he would be making more money in the airline business than ever before.

If Orville didn't consider you daft, the airline president would certainly call the men in the white coats.

Why this analogy? Because the space enterprise is going to create something just as complex, expensive, and big in your lifetime when it comes to space transportation. You'll be able to take your grandchildren down to the spaceport to watch the 3:15 flight leave the Supra Pacific Station with a load of people to work on SPS-57.

And you will be seeing only the Earth-based portion of the system. There is more of it in space, much more, because the Earth-to-orbit segment is only the first step into the Solar System.

It may turn out to be more economical and more efficient to lift some payloads off the Earth's surface and to a staging point in low-Earth orbit about 150 miles up where the payloads are transferred to deep-space vehicles that operate always in space and never land on any planet or moon. Or it may be better to loft other cargoes and/or people directly to the geosynchronous orbit 22,200 miles above the Earth where all the comsats, metsats, infosats, orbital antenna farms, and SPS units are located. Initially, space factories producing unique space materials will probably be located in low-Earth orbits where it is easier and faster to get to them to re-stock, change shifts, make repairs, and remove the finished products for shipment back down to Earth.

So the space transportation system is going to see a plethora of deep-space ships of various sorts. Some will be manned. Some will be robots operating under remote control or under the commands of an on-board computer . . . or a combination of both.

There will be space tugs that will haul payload containers out of the shuttles and propel them to different orbits.

There will be inter-orbit transfer ships that will take people from one orbit to another.

In the year 2000 when three of the segments of the space enterprise—communications, products, and energy—really begin to get moving in earnest, the space transportation system is going to blossom in all directions to handle the demands for transferring people and cargoes around in the Earth-Moon system. In the 21st Century, the space transportation system is going to grow even more as entrepreneurs finance the space pioneers who will return to the Moon to utilize the raw materials there and who will journey outward to the planetoid belt to tap the incredible Golconda of raw materials where there is practically no gravity well.

We need no super new rocket propellants to do this; we can do it with two of the most common elements in the Solar System: hydrogen and oxygen. We don't need to use nuclear rockets, although nuclear rockets would certainly improve performance. We don't need solar sails, although we will probably use solar sails (and other low-thrust propulsion systems such as ion rockets) for unmanned payload ships where you don't really care how long they are in transit as long as there are enough of them in transit at any one time to insure a constant delivery schedule. We can get hydrogen and oxygen for rocket propellants anywhere in the inner Solar System where we can locate rocks and use solar energy to rip the hydrogen and oxygen out of them.

The raw materials are there, as we will later see.

Using the technology developed for the SPS system, we can have electric power wherever we go and wherever there is enough sunlight to tap . . . which means we can probably go out to the orbit of Jupiter where it may be possible to utilize the internal energy of Jupiter itself.

We do lack one important item to permit us to operate a long-term, deep-space transportation system and its accompanying deep-space facilities: a closed-cycle life support system.

Thus far in space, we have been able to take along all the oxygen and food that we required. Water is no problem; our metabolism produces water as a by-product of cellular combustion in our bodies, and we exhale it as well as perspire it away. But in the 1980s we will have to develop a true closed–cycle system where we recycle everything possible. Closed–cycle life support systems have been designed, built, and tested here on Earth. Dr. George Morgenthaler, now Vice-President of Martin–Marietta, had one such system working in a Denver lab in 1959. I remember well being talked into drinking a glass of water that had been recycled from human urine. It tasted just like ordinary tap water. But building laboratory test units on Earth is a far different thing than building them for use in space where they *must* work. We can build closed-cycle life support systems, and we will. We are just going to have to learn how to do it in space in the 1980 decade . . . and it should have top priority.

However, if we are to progress rapidly beyond the stage of the NASA Space Shuttle, there are going to have to be some changes made in social organizations here on Earth. NASA has proven itself to be an outstanding government research and development operation; they have the people, the facilities, and the organization to do an excellent job of space exploration and high-risk development of advanced space hardware. NASA has a unique and successful working relationship with the aerospace industry. NASA has been successful at exploration and R & D. They should be encouraged and permitted to continue doing just that.

NASA should not be permitted to become the operating agency for a space transportation system. Unfortunately, as this is being written, this is exactly what is happening. But don't blame the people at NASA; they are trying to save their jobs and their organization because nobody has told them to proceed beyond the Space Shuttle. In fact, the word has come down from the Executive Office of the President to "fully exploit the capabilities of the Space Shuttle before taking on any new large projects."

This is an incredible *non sequitur* on the part of the administration. It's like saying, "Okay, you've now got a fleet of trucks, but we won't give you any money to build roads or to establish industries that the truck fleet can serve. First, you've got to utilize your truck fleet to its utmost."

The very best thing that could happen in the next five years is for a private organization to take over the operation of the Space Shuttle, allowing NASA to go back to the kind of work they have proven they do best: exploration and technical R & D.

Yes, there are problems posed by the military utilization of the Space Shuttle. There are some military payloads that will be highly classified such as powerful reconnaissance satellites used to verify the SALT agreements. But there should be no reason why the military should balk at having the Space Shuttle flown by crews from a civilian contractor; they have lots of highly classified contracts with civilian contractors. In fact, some of the nation's airlines already have such contracts and perform services for the military that go far beyond the occasional contract use of a Boeing 747.

There is nothing that prevents a Space Shuttle crew from having Top Secret clearances to permit them to fly missions carrying military payloads.

And, if it gets right down to the lickin' log, there is nothing that would prevent a contract between the military and the civilian operator that would allow a military crew to fly a Shuttle on a particularly sensitive mission.

The important thing is to get NASA out of the Space Shuttle operations activity as quickly as possible so they can get busy immediately with the design and development of the Space Shuttle's successor. After all, the Space Shuttle is designed to be worn out by 1990. To replace it at even that date, work has got to start *soon*. To come up with the interim Heavy–Lift Launch Vehicles of the late 1980s, work should already be under way. To some extent, it already is.

It is of interest to note that the Boeing Company has already stated that it wishes to take over Space Shuttle operations from NASA. Furthermore, Boeing wants to buy some more Space Shuttle Orbiters from Rockwell International, the company that builds them. It would not be at all surprising in the 1980 decade to see both Boeing and Rockwell building Space Shuttles . . . and operating them themselves. Rockwell International has already come out with the flat prediction that they intend to be the first company to show a profit from a product made in space by space processing. We will then be in a situation similar to the domestic airlines circa 1925–1928. General Aviation Corporation in St. Louis manufactured the Dutch Fokker aircraft under license and also had an interest in an airline called Transcontinental & Western Air (TWA) which, naturally, flew Fokker airliners. Boeing had a subsidiary, Boeing Air Transport, which had merged National Air Transport with Varney Airlines to form United Airlines; United naturally operated Boeing-built aircraft. This arrangement and others were broken up by President Franklin D. Roosevelt and the Department of Justice in 1934 under what was basically an anti–trust action. When the smoke cleared and the dust settled, both TWA and United emerged as separate entities no longer controlled by airplane manufacturers.

This bit of history is intended only to give you some perspective on what might transpire in the space transportation business during the next ten years. In other words, it has happened before and it may happen again. History may not repeat itself exactly, but its *patterns* may repeat themselves.

For the same reason, I would consider it highly unlikely that existing airlines would become space transportation operators. It is doubtful that we will see the Pan Am world, the American stooping eagle, or the Continental golden tail on a space shuttle. The stagecoach companies did not expand into the canal barge business. The canal companies started out in the railway business, but didn't last very long. Railway companies did not get into airlines (in spite of the fact that there was a railroad called Seaboard Air Lines that had absolutely nothing to do with airplanes). But it could happen, and it might happen, so don't count it out.

Right at this moment at the opening of the 1980 decade, space transportation is in an analogous position to the commercial airlines in the 1920s. A successful space transportation vehicle, the NASA Space Shuttle, is about to show everyone that it can be done. The need to fill the Shuttle and use its capability will create the first experimental space manufacturing operations and permit the first in-space experiments with SPS components. The availability of the Shuttle is now driving its customers. NASA is operating in a buyer's market. The success of some of the 30 dedicated payloads already scheduled and some of the more than 300 Getaway Specials will, by 1985, be driving the space transportation market. It will have turned around into a seller's market, and there is likely to be a shortage of orbital weight-lifting capability. This has already happened within the past 20 years with expendable converted military ballistic missiles used as space launch vehicles.

The most important thing about space transportation systems is that we *can* do it if we *want* to do it. We can build systems that will reduce costs to $10 per pound in Earth-orbit. We can build closed-cycle life support systems. We can transport people comfortably and reliably from Point A to Point B in space, and we can keep them alive there. We either have the technologies or can get them. And we must be ready, willing, and able to move quickly once the Space Shuttle proves out everything we are talking about in discussing the space enterprise. We must be thinking not only about the technologies involved, but also the government policies and regulations that would permit America to expand its worldwide success in commercial aviation into an overwhelming success in space transportation systems. We are not the only ones privy to the technology; the Japanese and the West Germans are hard on our heels and have already made significant inroads into American domestic aircraft markets. They can and will do the same in space transportation, given the opportunity to do so by our failure of will or nerve.

Please remember one thing very clearly: A space transportation system is not the reason to go into space, and it is not the entire space enterprise. Space transportation is an ancilliary *service* to the space enterprise just as railroads, trucks, and airplanes provide services to Earth-based industry. You don't build space transportation systems and then go looking for customers . . . or you'll go badly broke very quickly. You build an industrial need coupled with a social need, and the space transportation system will then be built to meet the requirements established by these needs. This is completely contrary to the way many people in the aerospace business have been brought up to think about space systems. It's high time that they held some seminars with their colleagues over in the commercial airliner divisions of their companies.

When you stop thinking about a space transportation system in isolation and begin thinking of it as a *service* to support activities of a profitable nature in space, the whole picture changes. It will result in the costs, reliability, regularity, and efficiency of space transportation systems falling right into line with every other type of transportation system we've ever developed.

CHAPTER SEVEN

It should become obvious to most readers by now that if the space enterprise is really going to grow beyond the Space Shuttle, a few large comsats, several small space factories producing a very limited number of highly specialized and very expensive space products, and a few SPS units intended to reduce a few peak loads at critical places on Earth, we are going to have to do something about raw materials.

Bringing raw materials up from the Earth, processing them in space, and either using them in space or returning them to the ground as special products rather defeats the long-range purpose of the space enterprise: quit raping Mother Earth for materials and start getting the raw materials somewhere else.

But there is something beyond this rather neat philosophical rationale. It's a matter of economics.

In order to bring up any amount of material from the Earth into low-Earth orbit, one must impart to that material a velocity of slightly more than 4.8 miles per second (25,500 feet per second) . . . and it's not only the speed that counts, but the direction as well because it must be a speed of about 4.8 miles per second in the direction and at the altitude you wish to maintain.

To impart this sort of velocity, you have to expend energy. Any time you expend energy, it costs money in terms of rocket propellant.

It would be much more economical to be able to get our raw material from some place in the Solar System where (1) energy to produce a change of velocity is abundant and therefore cheap, and/or (2) the gravity field is less, thereby requiring less velocity and less energy.

For the purposes of this discussion and several that will follow in later chapters, think of the Earth as being at the bottom of a very deep well or funnel-shaped hole. This hole represents the Earth's gravity field. It can be thought of as a "gravity well" with the Earth at the bottom of it.

If you stand on the Earth and throw a rock right straight up the sides of the funnel, it will climb all the way up the well and over the edge at the top—*if* you throw the rock with a velocity of 7 miles per second. This is the "escape velocity" of the Earth.

Up at the top of the Earth's gravity well is a relatively "flat" gravitational surface that is finally dimpled by the presence of the Moon with its gravity well about 1 mile per second deep. If you throw your rock up the side of the Earth's gravity well with enough velocity to go over the edge, and if you throw it in the right direction toward the Moon's gravity well, the rock will roll into the Moon's gravity well and impact the lunar surface at something more than a mile per second.

If you want to put something like a satellite or an SPS at a definite distance from the Earth part way up the sides of the gravity well, you must give it enough velocity to get it as high up the gravity well as you want it, then give it some sideways velocity so that it

whirls around and around on the "surface" of the
gravity well.

The accompanying illustration shows this a lot better than several hundred words.

Of course, the gravity wells of the Earth and the
Moon are only dimples on the huge gravity well of the
Sun, which in turn includes gravity well dimples for
all the major planets and planetary satellites.

Getting from one place to another place in the Solar
System is like getting from one point to another point
in the Earth-Moon gravity well system: it's a matter of
both speed and direction, which amounts to a matter
of energy, which relates to cost.

Therefore, if you're going to get your raw material
for space industry from a cheaper location, you have
to find a location with a lower velocity budget. You get

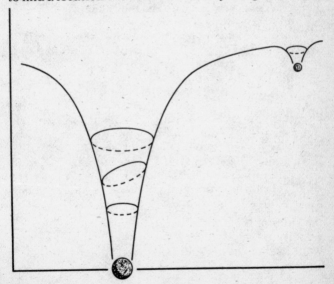

your rocks off smaller celestial bodies with weaker gravity fields and therefore shallower gravity wells.

The Solar System is *not* a matter of *distance*; it's a matter of *velocity* and *time*. Most of us have been born on planet Earth with an orientation that is Earth-centered, and we tend to think of the Solar System in terms of distances; some of us, on the other hand, have been trained to think of the Solar System in terms of velocities and times. There's a running battle going on with the news media, who love to quote the tremendous distances in the Solar System because they are such sensational numbers, truly astronomical in size. The next time you read a news report gushing about how terribly far it is—millions of miles, after all!—to Mars or the planetoid belt, please help yourself to a rather large portion of sodium chloride (salt) and remember that distance isn't the main factor; it's velocity and time that count.

In order to find a cheaper source of raw materials, we're going to go prospecting around the Solar System. We are already doing so. Our *Pioneers*, *Voyagers*, *Veneras*, *Mariners*, and *Vikings* are giving us our first look at the wealth of raw materials that is out there.

I can already hear the environmentalist groups sneering at me: "His capitalistic masters have already despoiled this planet, and now he wants to ruin the whole Solar System with his profit–seeking, exploitive destruction!" You bet I do! And my capitalistic "masters" are millions of ordinary, solid American citizens of all types who hold shares of common stock in companies big and small all over this country. I want to exploit the Solar System rather than continue to exploit our home planet. If we don't, we can expect to regress into a pre-industrial age where we don't ex-

ploit anything; in that situation, nine out of ten of you
are going to have to die so that there will be enough to
go around. Shall we draw straws for the honor, or shall
we shag our tails and try to "exploit" the Solar System
instead? If we do it right, we can have our cake and eat
it too. Either fish or cut bait, buddy, but don't stand
around yammering in my ear about how "evil" all of
this is. You've got the luxury of having the time to
yammer and picket and scheme because somebody
else happens to be doing your work for you . . . and I
notice that none of you appear to be starving . . .

Thus far in all of our history, we have had
only one planet to work with. It has an equatorial
diameter of about 7,926 miles. It has a mass of
6,588,000,000,000,000,000,000 tons. It has a surface
area of 196,938,800 square miles, about 70% of which
is covered by liquid dihydrogen oxide, the only known
planet in the Solar System where the liquid form of
this highly corrosive and abrasive chemical exists in
the free state. It is covered with a very thin layer of
cancerous-like material called "life." There is even
some speculation that there may be intelligent life on
Earth. We do know that three forms of intelligence exist on Earth: animal intelligence, human intelligence,
and military intelligence.

Some people believe we've already used up this
planet. We haven't used it up by any means, but we
may have misused it somewhat in our drive for survival. There has been a lot of discussion in engineering
circles about the possibility of "terraforming" other
planets in order to make them Earth-like; in the next
500 years, we are going to be given the opportunity to
try this by terraforming Earth.

Now we are about to venture out of the house that

has been our home during our childhood. We are about to go poking around our own back yard, the Solar System. And what a fine back yard it is!

Instead of one planet, we now have an average-sized middle–aged star, eight other planets, 34 major planetary satellites, four major satellite-sized planetoids, more than 40,000 planetoids, thousands of comets, and millions of meteoric chunks of rock.

The planets Mercury and Mars, plus the Moon, have a total surface area almost twice that of the land area of Earth! Mars alone has nearly the land surface area of Earth.

Thus, we are not talking about a Solar System consisting of Earth, the Sun, and some assorted bits of rocky sky junk.

There are whole planets out there, some of them as extensive in area as our home planet and some of them with much shallower gravity wells than our Earth.

In the words of Delos D. Harriman, "This is the biggest real estate deal since the Pope carved up the New World."

We will not initially get our raw materials from other planets. It's too expensive in terms of the depths of their individual gravity wells.

But we can consider the Moon with a gravity well only one-sixth as deep as Earth's, making it considerably less expensive to lob raw materials off of it. And, because the Moon has no sensible atmosphere to speak of (except what our Apollo landings left there from outgassing metals and propellant tanks), it will be possible to launch raw materials horizontally off the Moon using an electrically driven catapult powered by solar energy. Dr. Gerard K. O'Neill has called this a "mass driver." But a large number of us have written science fiction stories for more than 40 years with lu-

A solar-powered catapult or "mass driver" built horizontally on the surface of the Moon is used to launch payloads at about 2 kilometers per second. Since the Moon has no atmosphere, the catapult can be built horizontally across the lunar surface. The payload emerging from the muzzle of the catapult is nothing but a blur.

nar catapults (and even Earth-based catapults) as part and parcel of our stories.

What kind of raw materials can we probably obtain from the Moon? Most people think that the Moon is a worthless hunk of rock. That depends upon how you look at it . . . and a lot of people today would be very happy if others would keep on thinking that way—enterprising people who are planning to get out there and do something with those worthless lunar materials before others find out.

We have only sampled the Moon on a most cursory basis. After a little over a century of careful, on-the-spot, foot-by-foot examination of the Earth, we are just beginning to learn something about its planetology. Geologists have to poke around into the nooks and crannies of the landscape. The Earth has roughly four times the land area of the Moon, and we have placed only 12 men on the surface of the Moon on a temporary basis for a matter of a few hours at a time in only six different locations. We know about as much about selenology (lunar planetology) as we would if we had landed only 48 men at 24 locations on Earth . . . and if only four of these men had been trained and educated geologists. (We have landed only one astronaut who has been trained in geology on the lunar surface, the Honorable Dr. Harrison H. Schmitt, Senator from New Mexico.)

How much would we know about the Earth under those circumstances?

How much would we really know about Earth if we had brought back only 840 pounds of randomly selected surface material?

That's all we have of lunar material to study, a mere 840 pounds. Some of this material has not been studied at all yet because there hasn't been enough time or enough money to examine every Moon rock. A great deal of this lunar material is stored away at the NASA Johnson Space Center in Houston, Texas for future selenologists to ponder. And this untouched Moon rock may have a completely different utility within 50 years: It will tell us what the Moon was like before we started to use it.

However, using modern laboratory devices and techniques such as mass spectrometers and nuclear magnetic resonance devices, scientists have been able to dissect a percentage of the lunar material we have in our possession. And what they have found is encouraging to those of us who want to utilize extraterrestrial materials.

The Apollo lunar samples appear to fall into four general categories. First, there are the basaltic rocks from the lunar plains. Secondly, there are the anorthosite basalts of the lunar highlands. Both types of basalts are basically silicas made up of silicon, oxygen, calcium, aluminum, and iron. The anorthosites are not only very old but also uncommon on Earth. The third type of lunar material discovered by Apollo astronauts has been given the appellation KREEP—K standing for potassium, REE for rare earth elements, and P for phosphorous—and is found primarily in the lunar lowland areas. Finally, there is a basaltic type of rock with a very high aluminum content that was found by the Apollo 16 astronauts in the Descartes region of the Moon.

All of this is very encouraging. On the Moon, we have already found aluminum, metallic nickel-iron (from ancient meteoric impacts), silicon, calcium, oxygen, potassium, and phosphorus. We have yet to find any concentrations of these materials to equal the ore lodes of Earth. But they are there. And they are at the bottom of a gravity well only a mile-per-second deep. Furthermore, because of the lack of a sensible lunar atmosphere, there is abundant solar energy available at 0.3 calories per square centimeter per minute.

With energy and the basic elements available, human beings will use technology to extract what they need from the Moon. It will be a new technology working with very low-grade ores in one–sixth gravity and no atmosphere, but with plenty of solar energy. Wherever people have energy and matter to work with, they can do things . . . and they will do them on the Moon.

This is not to say that we know everything there is to

know about the Moon. We will know much more in 50
years' time when people go up there to crawl around
the moonscape looking for more concentrated lunar
ores. They may not be there, but I would not be willing
to bet that they are not.

We are pathetically provincial when it comes to the
field of planetology. We have known only one planet,
and we haven't yet known that one very well as should
be evident from some of the localized damage we've
managed to inflict upon it. We are just beginning to
realize how terribly provincial we really are, and
every space probe we send out tells us how little we
really do know. And even though people are not standing on Mars or circling Jupiter, the data from the *Mariners*, *Pioneers*, *Vikings* and *Voyagers* is not cold and
useless scientific information. In the company of some
of the world's finest science-fiction authors, science reporters, space artists and planetary scientists, I have
experienced the electrifying excitement of watching
the television monitors at the Jet Propulsion Laboratory in Pasadena, California as a picture came back
line by line from the surface of Mars or as a photograph of Io or Ganymede built up from a *Voyager*
swinging around Jupiter. If this exciting data told us
nothing else, it told us that the other bodies of the Solar System are not only different from the Earth but
also wildly more different than we had ever dreamed.

If the Moon lacks certain badly needed raw materials, we are most certain to find these raw materials
in the planetoid belt that exists between the orbits of
Mars and Jupiter. There are an estimated 40,000
pieces of rock ranging in size from a few hundred feet
in diameter up to major planetoids larger than Man-
hattan Island. In fact, four planetoids are as large as
some planetary satellites: Ceres, 477 miles in diame-

Unmanned payloads from space factories, "space box cars," will be landed on Earth using an umbrella-like "drag brake" to slow them down. Here, a load is just beginning entry into the atmosphere. (No specific location)

ter; Pallas, 306 miles in diameter; Juno, 127 miles in diameter, and Vesta, 244 miles in diameter.

The 40,000-plus planetoids are distributed in lumpy groups in a belt in the plane of the ecliptic of the Solar System that is 340 million miles broad between the orbits of Mars and Jupiter.

Getting to the planetoid belt from low-Earth-orbit takes roughly the same amount of energy in the form of velocity change as to go from low-Earth-orbit to lunar orbit—about 12,000–13,000 feet per second—which is far less than the 25,500 feet per second it takes to get to low-Earth orbit from the surface of the Earth. Therefore, it should be half again as expensive to get

to the planetoids as it is to get into space from the
Earth in the first place. Again, it must be emphasized
that it is *not* the distance that is important. With a
closed-cycle life support system that will come out of
space manufacturing and SPS programs in the 1990
decade, even a journey of a year or more out to the
planetoid belt is not impossible for human beings; it's
just very boring.

As astronaut Walter Schirra once remarked, para-
phrasing an ancient bit of humorous aviation wisdom,
space travel amounts to hours and days of boredom
punctuated by moments of sheer terror.

Once we get to the planetoid belt—which is easier
and cheaper than going to Mars because of the almost
total lack of gravity wells in the planetoid belt—what
will we find there?

Rocks.

Lots of rocks. Big rocks. Little rocks. Stones. Peb-
bles. Boulders. And some of them bigger than cities.

What are the planetoids made of?

We don't know yet. We'll find out when we get there
and we'll tell you when we get back . . . after having
staked our claims on the most valuable ones.

(Somebody is certain to bring up the legalistic point
that the "Moon and the planets and the planetoids are
the common property of all mankind." Very well, let
"all mankind" participate in providing the capital
grub stake to go out there, let "all mankind" participate in the dangers of exploring out there, and let "all
mankind" sweat and toil and possibly die in the process of extracting valuable raw materials from these
extraterrestrial resources. Under those conditions, do
you think it could be done? Hells bells, the United
States government alone cannot even run a satisfac-
tory postal service or passenger railroad system, much

less something as complex as mining extraterrestrial resources! And look at how well the world in general is handling the petroleum extraction business right now. Do you want to turn over control of the Solar System to such collective bungling?)

We can take a guess at what we will find in the planetoid belt, based upon some guesses as to why there is a planetoid belt there instead of a fifth planet (which has been given the sobriquet, quite unofficial, of "Vulcan"; sorry, Mister Spock).

The planetoid belt may either be the pieces of a planet that (a) never formed out of the primordial ejecta from the Sun in the early eons of the Solar System's creation because of the gravitational pull of the giant planet Jupiter, or (b) that loosely formed and then came apart under the gravitational pull of Jupiter. Jupiter is such a large planet that it contains more mass than all the other planets of the Solar System put together. About 71.6% of the planetary mass of the Solar System is the planet Jupiter. It is large enough that its gravitational field has probably compressed matter at its core almost to the point where thermonuclear ignition could take place. If Jupiter were just a little bit larger, the Solar System might have two suns, Jupiter becoming a very small star. If the Solar System were viewed from a distance of several light years—say from another star system—it might appear to consist only of two bodies: Sol and Jupiter. Thus, the gravity field of Jupiter could well have created the planetoid belt by preventing a planet from coming together or by pulling apart a proto-planet in the early days of the Solar System billions of years ago.

If that is the case, we may have a planet all cut up and waiting for us to haul away.

It may contain chunks of planetary core such as the

nickel-iron of Earth's core. It may contain only rocks
from the mantle and crust of the proto-planet, which
are also valuable.

We can make a good guess at the composition of the
planetoids by looking at the composition of the various types of meteors that fall to Earth and have been
picked up and analyzed. Only two general types of meteorites have been discovered. One type is made from
nickel-iron—planetary core material. They are made
up of iron and nickel . . . period. We have found them
on the surface of the Moon, too. And we find them all
over Earth. I have picked up small pebble-sized nickel-
iron meteorites on the slopes of the Barringer Meteor
Crater in Arizona (when it was still permitted). That
meteor crater was caused by the impact of a nickel-
iron meteorite about 80 feet in diameter. It was probably one of the smaller "close approach planetoids"
that have orbits of high eccentricity. Such close approach planetoids are fewer in number than the mob
out in the planetoid belt itself, and they swing in orbits
as close to the Sun as the orbit of Mercury and as far
from the Sun as the orbits of the outer gas–giant
planets Uranus and Neptune.

If even a small percentage of the rocks in the planetoid belt are nickel-iron, they will provide us with a
very large source of these materials for years to come.
A nickel-iron planetoid a mere one-mile in diameter
would contain 33 billion tons of materials, enough to
supply the steel needs of the United States for more
than 200 years.

The second type of meteorite that falls to the Earth's
surface is the rocky or "chondrite" type. The majority
of meteorites are chondrites. Their composition appears to be reasonably uniform from one to the next. If
the planetoid belt contains mostly chondrite-type

rocks, it's still nothing to weep about. Chondrites contain more than 13% metals such as iron, aluminum, magnesium, manganese, and titanium. The remainder of the chondrite material is silicates and oxides of the alkali metals. They are a source of oxygen. They also contain a fraction of a percent of water, which gives us a supply of hydrogen.

A one-mile diameter chondrite planetoid would provide us with a seven week supply of raw iron for the United States.

But the planetoid belt is such a long way away! That was the same sort of thinking that caused the collapse of the New England shipping industry in the 19th Century: "Why should we worry about things that are happening out in the Middle West? Chicago is a long way away. Our interests are here in New England!"

It isn't the distance that counts. It's the velocity and the time.

The planetoid belt offers a unique situation for obtaining extraterrestrial materials: there is practically no gravity well to overcome if you want to move extraterrestrial materials from the planetoid belt to anywhere else in the Solar System, including the Earth–Moon system. Right now, we move 60,000 tons of Mesabi Range iron ore at a crack in Great Lakes ore carrier ships. But we don't need spaceships in which to move chunks of planetoid iron. We can move mile-diameter planetoids if we wish. Give one a gentle shove in the right direction with a rocket motor. You don't have to shove it very hard with a lot of thrust if you've got a long-duration rocket engine to work with. Likewise, you can punch it very suddenly with a small nuclear bomb. It doesn't make any difference how you do it as long as you change its velocity by only a few hundred feet per second in the right direction at the

An important source of raw materials for the Twenty-First Century will be the planetoid belt. Shown here is a planetoid mining operation bringing planetoid materials up from a large open pit mine where they are being loaded in a manned ore freighter built with modular technology.

right time. Several hundred days later, it shows up where you want it—in the Earth-Moon system, or anywhere else. Another application of thrust slows it up and puts it in any orbit that you want so that you can work on it. If you want the iron for use in building an SPS, put the rock in Earth geosynch orbit. If you want the metal for constructing a space habitat at the Earth-Moon Lagrangian position, put the rock there. If you want it for use in building something on the Moon, put it in lunar orbit. And if you want it to fulfill an order for iron or steel on Earth, put it in low-Earth orbit and smelt it, form it, forge it, and refine it in space where you've got solar energy to work with.

If you build a solar energy concentrator, a mirror, about 300 feet in diameter, it will concentrate enough energy at its focus to vaporize more than 24 pounds of copper per second. The easiest, quickest, and cheapest way to make this solar concentrator is to blow a plastic bubble and coat one hemisphere with vapor-deposited silver or aluminum—preferably aluminum from the Moon or the planetoid belt.

But we can't start thinking about the "far out" possibility of utilizing extraterrestrial materials until we have worked our way step by step through the early phases of the space enterprise—the Space Shuttle, the early space products, advanced communication systems, and some sort of SPS system. Only then will we have developed the attendant technologies to the point where it will not only seem natural to go back to the Moon and out to the planetoid belt for extraterrestrial materials, but an absolute economic necessity that we do so.

If we can get extraterrestrial materials in very large amounts from the Moon and from the planetoid belt—or even from some of the close–approach planetoids—

A solar smelter at work in Earth orbit where a 100-meter mirror has concen-planetoid metals.

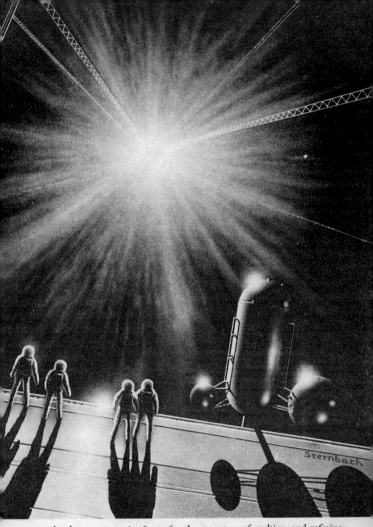

trated solar energy at its focus for the purposes of melting and refining

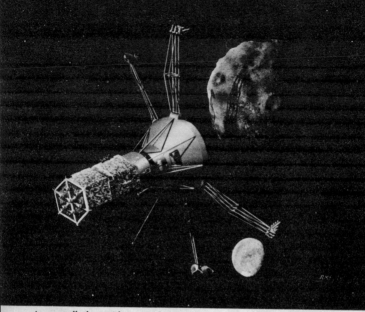

As a small planetoid approaches Earth at the end of its journey from the planetoid belt, a manned "locomotive" completes rendezvous and prepares to secure the planetoid prior to changing velocity to insert the load into an Earth orbit near an orbital steel mill.

with less energy than hauling them up from the Earth, the space entrepreneurs will opt for the more economical way to do the job. We will need those extraterrestrial materials to build cheaper SPS units to supply not only the needs of Earth, but the increasing needs of the space enterprise. We will need those cheaper extraterrestrial materials to build many of the very large structures that will be required and that are possible in space to house the activities of the space enterprise.

These capabilities will grow out of the space transportation systems developments of the 1980s and 1990s.

By the first decade of the 21st Century, some members of the human race will be returning to the Moon, this time to stay and to develop the natural resources there. Other human pioneers will be on their way toward the planetoid belt, searching out the Mesabi Range of the Solar System. And by the year 2010, we can anticipate seeing products not only made in space, but made from materials obtained in space. By 2025, it may be cheaper to obtain these basic raw materials from space than from the Earth.

If you want to see an end to open-pit mining on Earth, and if you want to halt the human suffering from death in the mines and miner's diseases such as black lung, the wisest course of action now and for the next quarter of a century is to support, work for, and participate in the real, workable solution: the space enterprise.

Because the further we get into the space enterprise, and the faster we can make it happen, the faster we will be able to stop the nukes and close the pits and start turning the Earth back into a garden planet.

Any alternative leads down a blind alley. Only the space enterprise with its open frontier offers a lasting and long-range solution.

A lunar mining base on the edge of Mare Crisium with a supply ship depart-
the lunar catapult installation which would appear only as a thin line run-

ing for the L-5 base. Not shown because of the small scale of the drawing is
ning across the maria if it were visible.

CHAPTER EIGHT

Up to now we've been thrusting madly along, discussing the space enterprise, what it entails, and what some of the potential returns may be—both monetary and social returns. But we have yet to address a central question of the space enterprise: Where and how are we going to get the money? After all, a very large capital investment will be required to establish space manufacturing facilities and even to pay for SPS units at $2000 per kilowatt installed. As a matter of fact, where do we find the capital to invest in such an immediate thing as Space Shuttle payloads and Getaway Specials?

One of the very first things that a space entrepreneur is going to have to learn is how to talk to bankers and other people with access to very large amounts of money. This is not an easy thing for most space entrepreneurs to do because they are so deeply engrossed in the beautiful technology, the great social payoffs, or the pure frontier adventure of the space enterprise.

A financier couldn't care less.

A financier has money because he knows how to make money. He invests his money in places that will provide him with the greatest return on his investment within a reasonable period of time and with a minimum amount of risk.

A financier who does a good job at this makes money for himself and for others as well, creating new jobs for people, and providing new opportunities for others. A financier who does a poor job at it does not remain a financier very long.

A financier can be a banker, investment counselor, personal investor, a corporate planner, or any businessman involved with the job of investing capital—money and human talents—in new ventures. He's going to put some of his money into investments that will pay off in a short period of time with low risk. He's going to put some capital into longer-term investments with low risk. And he may have some crapshooting money that he uses for long-term and high-risk ventures where there is less chance of a return on investment but a greater amount of return if the venture does happen to pay off.

Right now, most financiers will take a flier with the communications/information segment of the space enterprise for one simple reason: This segment has a proven track record. Comsat's net income per share for the first quarter of 1979 was $1.49 per share. The risk is low and the return on investment is near-term.

But when you begin to talk to financiers about space processing, to say nothing of an SPS system, you are going to get a very interesting reaction. I have talked with a lot of businessmen from companies big and small, from Fortune 500 corporations down to individually owned companies, over the past several years. In general, the reactions have been about the same.

"It's going to take a lot of money. The risk is pretty high because you really don't know very much about

space processing yet. Your data is too soft, and a lot of
things that you take for granted are really highly con-
jectural. Space transportation costs are too high by a
factor of ten or more. And it will be ten to 15 years
before I can possibly reach a break-even point, much
less a return on investment. In the meantime, I've got
better places to put my R & D money, places where the
risk is lower and the possibility of a new and profitable
product is higher."

"SPS? The concept sounds very good. Of all the energy alternatives we've heard about, this one seems to
be the most acceptable from an environmental point
of view. Furthermore, since it uses renewable resource, it means that we won't be faced with fuel allocations ten years down the line. If we can put up an
SPS for $2000 per kilowatt installed, then we are very
much interested. But the technology is not proven
and, therefore, the risk is very high."

"We couldn't amass the amount of capital required.
In order to finance the portion of the space enterprise
that is of interest to us, we'd have to get together with
several other firms and some financial houses. If we
did that, our attorneys tell us that we'd be deep into
an anti-trust violation immediately. The federal government just wouldn't let us put together the capital
base to carry it out, and it would therefore be under-
capitalized and subject to certain failure."

"We just couldn't do it right now because none of
your proposals would weather the rigors of our corporate new venture evaluation program. We must
subject all new proposals for new products to this
evaluation because we are working with stockholders'
money and we are answerable to them through the
Board of Directors."

"We really don't have any interest in such far-out

Buck Rogers stuff right now, but I wish you'd keep us informed of developments that might be of interest to us. If our competitor becomes involved, I would think that we'd probably want to take another closer look at this."

These are paraphrases of things that I have been told since 1977 by American businessmen, managers, financiers, corporate officers, and corporate planners, all of whom were not involved in any way with the aerospace industry. Therefore, this feedback can be considered to be a fairly representative reaction of the core of American domestic industry to the space enterprise.

Note that salient points are made over and over again: (a) the capital requirements are very high; (b) the data base is too soft to permit a rational business decision to be made; (c) the return-on-investment is a long way in the future; and (d) the risk is considered to be very high.

"The whole picture might undergo a drastic change," I have been told on several occasions by different businessmen, "if the government were to assume some of the risk or if there were some way to spread the risk without running afoul of the many rules, regulations, and laws of the IRS and the Justice Department."

Risk.

Capital requirements.

Long payback times.

Insufficient data.

These items have been the bane of American business for at least two centuries and were also among the factors that faced the earliest colonists in the New World.

Historically, every time a situation with these characteristic problems has arisen in the past, two things have taken place: (a) the government has developed a unique government-business arrangement to reduce the risk, and (b) one or more new forms of social organization have been invented to share the risk and to permit the accumulation of the required capital resources.

And, to the surprise of nobody who has been interested in the space enterprise, it is happening again right now just as history forecast it would.

The interest and intervention of the federal government of the United States in business and commerce hasn't always been restrictive and regulatory. The federal government has a long history of assisting American free enterprise.

One of the first acts of Congress was the funding of the National Road across the Allegheny Mountains so that the farmers of the Ohio River Valley could ship their grain to the markets on the East Coast; without the road, the farmers were forced to convert their grain into the more easily transportable grain alcohol . . . and there was a stiff federal tax on it which caused the Whiskey Rebellion. Thus, without stretching one's imagination very much, it isn't difficult to see that the Whiskey Rebellion was the original reason for the Interstate Highway System of today.

Early in the 19th Century, the federal government provided loans and guarantees for the construction of the extensive canal system of the East Coast, "those expensive ditches" in the lexicon of one of their critics who would probably be in the environmentalist camp today. But canals were the only method of transporting heavy loads before the advent of the railroads.

When the capital requirements and subsequent financial risks associated with building extensive railroad systems became exceptionally large, the federal government stepped in again. The Pacific Railroad Act of 1862 was enacted in the midst of the Civil War. The Act provided for land grants, government bonds for each mile of track laid, government guaranteed loans, and a government–chartered corporation called the Union Pacific Railroad Company. The Honorable Henry Wilson of Massachusetts said in the United States Senate at that time, "I would sink a hundred million dollars into opening a railroad and do it most cheerfully, and think that I had done a great thing for my country. What are 75 or a hundred million dollars in opening a railroad across the central regions of this continent that shall connect the people of the Atlantic and Pacific and bind us together?" (The hundred million dollars of 1862 money would be equivalent to 75 *billion* 1979 dollars.)

When the agricultural and industrial heartland of America in the Midwest began to grow, prosper, and mature in the late 19th Century and early 20th Century, it needed new markets. America's Mississippi River Basin emptied into the Gulf of Mexico, and the marketplace it had to look toward was not Europe but the Orient. The result was the Spooner Act of 1902 which authorized the construction of the Panama Canal and set up the Panama Canal Company as a wholly owned government corporation, the first such in history. And the tremendous output of America's heartland then had a water trade route directly to and across the Pacific Ocean.

Two other examples of congressional action to assist industry changed America beyond all possible forecasting. The Morrill acts set up the land grant colleges which, in turn, raised the educational level of our farmers and engineers which, in turn, made our broad prairies into the breadbasket of the world. The Reclamation Act of 1904 not only encouraged the development of American lumber and paper industries, but gave birth to whole new recreational industries and created vast new farmlands and new shining cities where only prairies and deserts had stood before. These two acts of Congress to assist American domestic industry raised the educational level of our people and created extensive conservation long before the environmentalists gained attention. Look at old glass-plate photographs of the American West; sparse saplings and scrub brush are visible in those photographs where verdant stands of timber exist today.

The United States postal service may be the object of considerable criticism today. But without its predecessor, the Post Office Department, it is exceedingly doubtful if the United States would be the world leader in commercial aviation today. It was the Kelly Act of 1925 that took the actual flying of the air mail out of the hands of the Post Office Department (who had been trying to fly the mail with a small and inadequate fleet of ancient Curtiss "Jennies" and De-Haviland "Flying Coffins") and put the transportation of air mail up for contract bid by commercial firms. Without these air mail contracts, the early airlines might not have survived. Today's major trunk airlines can trace their roots directly back to those first 1925 air mail contracts.

American industrial output today moves by ship, by rail, by air, and by road. Congress gave the impetus to the trucking industry through the Highway Revenue Act of 1956 which established the interstate highway system and its financing trust fund. There was more behind the need for the interstate highways than personal or commercial travel, because this highway network responded to defense needs as well. It has been the greatest road building program in all history. It took the Roman Empire about 500 years to build 50,000 miles of narrow, rock-surfaced roads. In a mere quarter of a century, Americans have more than equaled that mileage with four-lane, high-speed divided interstate highways.

Even in the area of space industrialization, we find an important historical precedent: The Communications Satellite Act of 1962. This set up the Communications Satellite Corporation with a government charter but with equity capital obtained from both the private sector and the communications carriers. It was done not only to distribute the risk, but to meet the requirements of the many international telecommunications treaties to which the United States is a party. And Comsat worked. It is not possible to determine the financial and intangible benefits that have accrued to the American people from the worldwide audio, video, and data transmission capabilities of communications satellites orbited by Comsat. And it is totally impossible to assess the long-range impact of instantaneous worldwide communications upon the political, economic and cultural aspects of human life on this planet. It is now possible to make a direct-dialed telephone call to 64 countries for less than $10 from any telephone in America . . . and there is now one telephone for every two Americans.

Thus, many historical precedents exist where the federal government has worked out a unique relationship with American business to permit business to become involved in long-range, high-risk, capital-intensive high-technology activities. And it is happening again today in the space enterprise.

If there is historic precedence for government help-

ing American industry, we don't necessarily have to
break new ground and try something totally different.
But will any of the solutions of the past contribute to
solving today's problems of the space enterprise? Perhaps so. Perhaps not. Let's take a look at a few possibilities.

I say a "few" because there are many. Rudyard Kip-
ling once advised us:
>"There are nine-and-sixty ways
>   Of writing tribal lays
>   And every single one of them is right!"

In other words, there is almost an infinite number of
different ways that we could set up a government/
business organization to finance and/or manage various aspects of the space enterprise. All of them would
probably work. But some of them would undoubtedly
work better than others.

There are two basic aspects to any organization:
ownership and *control*. They are two different things.
It is possible to own something without controlling it;
if you own shares of common stock in a corporation,
you may own part of the company but you really don't
control it because that is done by the executive officers
of the firm. And the opposite is true: you can control
an organization without owning it; just work for it in
a position of authority.

Part and parcel of this dualism is the fact that financing or providing money for an operation or organization is quite separate and different from managing and controlling it. To a great extent, "financing"
can be equated with "ownership" while "managing"
is equivalent to "control."

The permutations and combinations of government
and private financing and management would, at first
glance, seem to create a matrix of four types of orga-

nizations: government financed and government managed; government financed and privately managed; privately financed and government managed; and privately financed and privately managed. But that is rather a simplistic matrix, one element of which is completely new, maybe unworkable, and riskier to try than any other approach: privately financed and government operated.

Actually, the various combinations do not create a box-like matrix but a continuous spectrum of organizational arrangements from total socialistic collectivism on the far left to complete *laissez faire* capitalism on the far right. There are obvious advantages and disadvantages to either extreme. And it is very interesting to discuss this matter with other people because their personal political-ideological bias immediately becomes patently evident.

However, when we begin to examine a number of different arrangements against a set of criteria consisting of characteristics that should be possessed by any organization involved in the space enterprise, a very large number of potential organizational forms drop out of the picture.

These organizational criteria are unique because we've never done anything like the space enterprise before. It's a series of business ventures in a totally new and different environment. To operate successfully in the space enterprise, any organization is going to have to have the following attributes—at least in the early years until it becomes "business as usual in the Solar System."

1. The ability to obtain the necessary capital, probably on a time-phased basis, to permit the complete implementation of whatever the project is up to the point where there is a return on investment. Under-

capitalization causes the failure of many business ventures, second only to lack of information and careful study prior to start-up.

2. Continuity, stability, and flexibility in order to react quickly and in an appropriate fashion to rapidly changing and fast-developing new technologies, some of which will not progress as forecast. The organization must remain committed to an overall long-range goal—for example, providing space-generated energy to Earth—regardless of the technology that is eventually worked out to do the job.

3. Appropriate distribution of both the risks and the benefits. Those who take the maximum risks should have the maximum share of the rewards.

4. Possibility of the broadest sort of participation in the financing and the return on investment. Acceptance by the public in the United States and abroad will be much higher if everyone who so desires can get a piece of the action.

5. Lack of obvious domination by either "big government" or "big business."

6. Ability to capitalize on spinoff technologies while at the same time protecting the technological advantages to be gained.

7. Minimum identification with military activities.

Now let us look at several suggested methods of organizing for the space enterprise, keeping these criteria in mind.

If the government does it all, there are going to be problems that are best summarized by the statement of a young space entrepreneur: "So you'd like to see space industrialization operated with the same efficiency and reliability as the U.S. Postal Service and Amtrak?" Total government control of both financing and management fail the criteria set forth above on all

counts. Necessary capital would come from tax revenues and would be totally dependent upon political
whims from year to year both in Congress and the
administration; the space program has suffered from
this already. Total government control will inevitably
result in a bureaucracy that would fail to meet Criterion #2; we have seen the result of this in the government program to harness fusion power. The inability
to meet the other criteria is obvious.

Existing American domestic business and industrial corporations can't meet all those criteria either.
As previously mentioned, anti-trust and SEC regulations prevent the accumulation of the required capital
of Criterion #1. Robert Poole pointed out during a discussion in San Francisco in October 1977 at the first
conference on space industrialization that there is
only one corporation in the world that combines the
attributes of possessing enough equity to finance a
space venture, has the ability to raise additional equity capital if necessary, can afford to take the risk and
lose without destroying the company, has a proven record of backing far-out technology beyond the current
state of the art, and possesses a group of executive officers and a board of directors that are young enough
and aggressive enough to see the whole thing through
to a 15 to 20–year return on investment. That corporation turns out to be Exxon Company.

We must therefore look at potential organizations in
the "gray area" of the spectrum between the right and
the left, searching for an optimum group of organizational set-ups that will permit government participation in reducing the high risks of the early period and
allow private enterprise to do an efficient job of operating and managing the space enterprise once the high
risk factors are eliminated.

Three approaches have come to light in the past several years, each of them a new and unique solution to the knotty problem.

Christian O. Basler, an attorney formerly with Western Electric, was asked by Dr. O'Neill to figure out an approach to financing an SPS system utilizing the private enterprise method of management. Basler is an expert in corporate law, especially with regard to anti-trust and Securities Exchange Commission regulations. He has proposed a unique organization called a "staging company." Basler has already incorporated International Satellite Industries, Inc., in the State of Delaware on August 3, 1978 organized on the staging corporation concept. This may best be summarized by quoting directly from the Synopsis of the Preliminary Prospectus of ISI, Inc., dated March 5, 1979:

"International Satellite Industries, Inc. is a new closed-end diversified management investment company. Its investment objective is to earn income to finance the research and development necessary to make space industrialization, including construction of solar power satellites, profitable for the company while maximizing the level of unrealized capital gains consistent with this objective. To the extent appropriate it will invest in equity securities of corporations it deems likely to profit from space industrialization. Until the Company has completed its third public offering and has net assets in excess of $35 million, it will invest solely in securities issued or guaranteed as to principal or interest by the United States.

"So long as it remains an investment company, the Company intends to spend substantially all of its income from investments on research and development. When in the opinion of the Company space industrial-

ization becomes economically feasible with the level
of assets then held, the Company intends, upon approval of holders of a majority of the Company's outstanding Common Stock, to cease to be an investment
company and to become an operating company engaged in space industrialization.''

Basler's staging corporation concept reverberated
like a thunderclap through the hundreds of people
who attended the conference on space industrialization sponsored by the American Astronautical Society
in San Francisco in October 1977. Here was a new approach to the financial problems of space industrialization. ISI, as it is now known, starts out as a pure
investment company with the full understanding that
the stockholders cannot expect an immediate return
on investment; all profits from the ISI portfolio will go
toward contracts with existing companies for research and development on aspects of space industrialization. At the same time, ISI will buy into the
common stock of those companies with whom it
places contracts because, if the R & D is successful, the
company will make money, its stock value will increase, and the ISI portfolio will increase in value.
When enough of the R & D problems have been solved,
ISI turns itself into an operating company to build
SPS units, for example. Or to manufacture some new
products in space.

Basler is an expert in anti-trust and securities regulations. At the time of this writing, his preliminary
prospectus has been filed with the SEC but the ISI reg-
istration certificate has not yet become effective. But
it will. There is nothing in the ISI prospectus that is
likely to cause any trouble with the SEC.

Basler's staging company offers a solution to two of
the major problems we have already discussed. One of

these is the sheer magnitude of the capital investment required for just the SPS system alone. The SPS system will probably cost in the neighborhood of $100 billion, which is only about 5% of the current annual federal budget. But it is more than the total assets of the world's largest corporation, AT&T, and about seven times the cost of the proposed natural gas pipeline from Alaska which, if built, would be the world's largest privately financed construction project to date. It's very obvious that the space enterprise cannot be financed by any existing corporation or any small consortium of companies from retained earnings. If the stockholders didn't revolt and throw out the Board of Directors of these companies, the SEC and the Department of Justice might want to have a very careful look at things.

The other problem solved by the staging company is the length of time—about 20 years—before a substantial payout appears possible.

The Basler staging company concept also addresses the "Catch-22" situation that has probably become apparent to most readers by this time: The risk is too high to allow you to spend the money to do the R & D that will reduce the risk to an acceptable level. The diversity of technologies required for the space enterprise is far beyond the capabilities of any one corporation in the world today. R & D expenses by individual corporations on the segments of the space enterprise relating to their line of business could not be justified because they would offer a profitable payback only in the context of a fully operating space enterprise. Existing corporations cannot combine into a joint venture or a consortium because stockholders probably would not wish to sacrifice earnings to the extent required and also because it couldn't be done without specific government approval and regulations to avoid existing anti-trust laws. After all, if a consortium is formed for all or part of the space enterprise, it's got to come up with an agreeable division of costs of production of the various systems involved, which means that their eventual prices are going to be based on these costs, which means "price fixing" to the federal government.

All of these facts were considered by Basler in formulating the staging company concept. It's new and it's different. It may encounter political resistance in some quarters not only because of its newness but also because it may threaten those who would like to see the space enterprise done in another way that promises them more power over people and money.

ISI meets nearly all of the criteria for evaluation of organizations, financing, and management of the space enterprise. Whether it will work or not depends upon a very large number of variables. But it deserves a chance, and it looks like it's going to get that chance. One thing for certain: The staging company concept deserves its place in the history of social organizations as an attempt to overcome the shortcomings of existing organizations in doing something totally new. I'd suspect that the staging company sounds as strange and risky today as did the very first incorporated trading company, the Merchant Adventurers of 1553 who attempted to establish a trade route by the Northwest Passage to Siberia. Or the Massachusetts Bay Company formed shortly thereafter. Progress into a new frontier always has created its unique new social organizations to handle the unique new problems. This is what is so exciting about Basler's staging company;

it may be the first of a whole new family of organizations which are created by and create (it's difficult to draw the line) the space enterprise.

Another unique organization for financing and managing long–term, high-risk ventures has been suggested by George F. Fredericks and Richard D. Stutzke. It is the "taxpayer stock corporation" which is a rather unique blend of government and private enterprise. It would work this way: The operation of this government chartered but privately operated corporation would receive its equity financing by earmarking a percentage of each individual's or corporation's income tax (or some other special tax) toward the issuance by the government of shares of common stock in a space industrialization corporation. The taxpayer then has the option of retaining the stock as a long-term investment or of selling the stock on the open market if he does not support the objectives of the corporation. The corporation would be under private control and would eventually pay dividends to its stockholders. Since the government acted only as a channel through which the equity capital passed, the corporation owes the government something equivalent to a broker's commission. Such a proposed taxpayer stock corporation would therefore be a government financed and privately managed organization.

If this offers any indication that many people are actively thinking about the space enterprise and how to finance and manage it, consider the fact that the matter has already been brought to the attention of Congress and that Congress has been working in close cooperation with businessmen, economists, technologists, and others interested in the space enterprise. And, lo and behold, *another* new social organization has arisen to cope with the problem. This is detailed in House Resolution 2337, 96th Congress, 1st Session, in the Space Industrialization Act of 1979 introduced by Congressman Don Fuqua. H.R. 2337 has, as of this writing, been the subject of hearings by the House Committee on Science and Technology. The Act would set up a Space Industrialization Corporation as a government chartered and government financed company run by a private-sector Board of Directors. It would be funded each year by Congress starting with a budget of $50 million. It would put this money into a Space Industrialization Trust Fund in the U.S. Treasury. Out of this Trust Fund, the Corporation would provide financial assistance to individuals and companies for research and development in the area of space processing. If a project fails, the individual or organization who received funding from the Space Industrialization Corporation would *not* have to pay back its grub stake, but it *would* have to submit a full and complete report of what it did and why the project failed; this is intended to keep others from "reinventing the wheel" or, as one Congressional staff member put it, to "keep others from inventing the square wheel."

If the supported project was a success and led to a profitable product, the Space Industrialization Corporation would be paid back by those to whom it staked, but paid back according to a predetermined agreement concerning how much, when, and with what return on investment for the Corporation. The Corporation must then deposit such paybacks in the Space Industrialization Trust Fund.

In due course of time, the Trust Fund is going to get large (hopefully) and government funding of the Corporation by annual budget requests will no longer be required. The Corporation has then become a self-sustaining operation.

There seems to be a general feeling that a Space Industrial Corporation would offer American domestic industry the relief from the problems of high risk associated with space processing. Some of the people testifying at the hearings, especially Dr. John F. Clark, felt that the Corporation should never engage in its own R & D work since that would put it in direct competition with those it was financing. Others felt that the Corporation should not be converted to a regular stock corporation once the Trust Fund became large enough to support its activities without subsidy from Congress; this, they felt, would cause the officers and directors of the Corporation to become overly conservative since they would have to begin thinking about providing their stockholders with a return on investment. If it were to remain a small, lean, lightly staffed government agency, it would be able to maintain its ability and willingness to back "far–out" projects in space processing and, eventually, other aspects of the space enterprise.

These three organizational concepts—the staging company, the taxpayer stock corporation, and the Space Industrialization Corporation—have all come about since 1976.

They tell us one thing: The space enterprise is considered to have enough potential to warrant the interest of people other than the usual space buffs. There is hard and serious work under way right now in an attempt to solve the problems of financing and managing the space enterprise. If the space enterprise were only a concept in the minds of a few advocates who wanted to perform neat technical tricks in space, one might be inclined to dismiss the whole affair. But it has turned into more than that in even five years' time.

Yes, the space enterprise is going to be risky.

Yes, it's going to be expensive—your gold teeth, your wife's jewelry, and your other shirt, plus whatever else you can put into hock.

Yes, it's likely to be a number of years before a payback becomes available.

But we are already coming up with the necessary new social organizations that will be required to finance it and to manage it.

We're going to do it.

CHAPTER NINE

Many readers may have come to the tacit assumption that the space enterprise will be an American accomplishment, with the primary benefits accruing to Americans. This is really not the case. We all labor under the assumption that the United States is and will remain the world leader in space technology.

Well, it isn't so now, and unless we get a move on, it won't be so in the future, either. The international involvement and impact of space industrialization even today may come as a surprise to many people.

At this moment, the worldwide gross annual revenue from activities in space exceeds a billion dollars.

Those segments of the space enterprise already in place in the communications area and planned in the materials processing area are strong and viable international and multi–national activities. Look at the data:

Twenty years after the launching of *Sputnik*, most of the world depends upon space systems for basic communications. Intelsat has over a hundred member nations. Thirty-nine nations have communications satellite ground stations capable of handling both communications and data transfer.

Twenty-four nations have space launch facilities. Fifteen of these nations have sub–orbital launch facil-

ities, nine are capable of launching into low-Earth orbit, and three of these have the capability to return a
payload from low-Earth orbit. Four countries have the
launch capability to put something into geosynchronous orbit. Seven nations own or operate Earth resources satellites. Thirteen nations have communications satellites in orbit. And five nations are involved
in materials processing in space.

The Europeans are deeply committed to the space
enterprise. Eurospace was formed in 1961 with 96 individual industrial organizations from 11 nations as
members along with 31 banks.

Japan has the capability with its own indigenous
launch vehicles to place almost one ton in geosynchronous orbit. Japan has not only developed its own
family of space launch vehicles but, following a trend
in their aviation industry of more than half a century,
it is building its own versions of foreign launch vehicles such as the U.S. *Delta* under license. Japan has
made a heavy commitment to space industrialization
in both government and industrial circles, and the
Japanese government is offering various types of support to Japanese industrial concerns involved in the
space enterprise.

Japan is not alone. In the Federal Republic of Germany, a group known as ANS (the Space Utilization
Working Group) has been formed by three West German corporations. The Bonn government has set up a
national payload center. No one would be greatly sur-
prised if the Federal Republic of Germany purchased
its own *SpaceLab* to be flown in the U.S. Shuttle; after
all, West Germany is one of the consortium of ten European nations building the *SpaceLab*.

The European Space Agency (ESA) is also hard at
work on an expendable launch vehicle called *Ariane*,

with which it intends to compete with the U.S. Space Shuttle in terms of cost per pound in the 1980s. The first launch is scheduled before the publication date of this book.

As this is being written, yet another two-man crew of cosmonauts is inhabiting the Soviet space station, *Salyut-6*, which is being resupplied automatically by *Progress* tanker craft to replenish oxygen, rocket propellants, and bring up the mail from home. The Soviets are conducting experiments in space processing in *Salyut-6* as this is being written. We know that they are engaged in experiments in making new alloys, growing crystals, and welding in vacuum. I seriously doubt if the Soviets would tell us exactly what they are doing and what their results are. Macy's doesn't tell Gimbel's. And we are, after all, in economic competition with them. At the moment, they may be gaining an important technological edge that will reveal itself as an economic edge in space processing. The Soviets have developed a workable—if unsophisticated and, to our spoiled technological eyes, primitive—space transportation system that is working on a regular basis. Furthermore, there are well-substantiated reports that the Soviets are now testing their version of a reusable shuttle; this will probably be smaller than our own Space Shuttle, but it may be of adequate size for Soviet needs. (Please recall that our Space Shuttle's size is based on required payloads to supply the space station for the now-defunct Manned Mars Landing Program.)

As a matter of fact, we must also look upon the Soviet Union as if it were USSR, Inc., because from the economic point of view that is exactly the way it acts. Having visited several Eastern European nations who labor under a communist/socialist political regime, I felt as though I were in one, big "company town" of the same sort that used to exist—albeit on a smaller scale—in the coal fields of West Virginia and Pennsylvania and the mining areas of New Mexico and Arizona. The company owns everything. Everyone works for the company. Everyone is in hock to the company store. The company is extremely paternalistic and brooks no dissension in the ranks. Everything is under tight control. And the Whole Outside World is the market and the competition. The old Anglo-American company town and the modern communist/socialist state differ only in degree, not in kind, (except you can't leave town). In spite of the USSR's lack of many internal niceties, it is perfectly capable of directing its productive and marketing energies into the external world at the expense of its own people, and it has done this over and over again. If the USSR gets a leg up on space processing—which it is now in the process of doing in *Salyut-6*—we can expect some competition there, but a different sort than many American firms are used to meeting.

We may have forgotten *Sputnik* in the wake of *Apollo-11*, but the Soviets haven't forgotten what it is like to be Number One. They are disturbingly close to holding that position right now, if they don't already hold it on the basis of our footdragging with Shuttle.

The People's Republic of China has launched their own satellite into near-Earth orbit using their own launch vehicle. It doesn't make any difference if the launch vehicle *was* a Chinese copy of a Russian development of the German V-2 rocket—the Chinese did it themselves. They have announced that they intend to have a manned capability in space before 1990 . . . their own vehicles, spacecraft, and orbiting space facilities.

It is quite obvious that the high-tech nations of the world and those that are aspiring to high-tech status in this century are fully aware of some of the potentials of the space enterprise; it would be surprising if they were not. The advocacy of the space enterprise in America would be more difficult if these other nations were not perking up and taking notice. We should pay particular notice to the interest in the space enterprise expressed by the Federal Republic of Germany and Japan. These are two systems based on private enterprise like our own. Like our own system, they are driven hard by the profit motive. Japan has the launch vehicle capability and the further ability to develop a space transportation system if it wants to expend the capital. Germany gave birth to the space rocket and has been the home ground of an upstart private space launch vehicle company called OTRAG, much to the consternation of the Soviet Union and some American aerospace companies.

The international aspect of the space enterprise is already creating considerable international competition in the communications satellite segment. Comsat does not make its own satellites; it contracts those to such firms as Hughes and TRW. In turn, these satellite builders must have things done on subcontract and buy components, because no single company in the world has the total expertise necessary to make everything that goes into a modern communications satellite. American firms are experiencing difficulties in getting certain communications satellite components such as momentum control wheels used to position and aim a communications satellite and, believe it or not, large solar power arrays that are folded up during launch and deployed once the satellite is in orbit. These are but two examples, and they were caused by

NASA's decision in the late 1960 decade to get out of communications satellite R & D activities because of budget cutbacks. This created a lack of stimulation of R & D in an emerging new technology where the old bugaboos of high risk and long payback times simply would not permit American corporate executives to expend their corporate funds in the area.

On the international scene, therefore, competition already exists in the high-tech cultures for the communications satellite business. There is an obvious competitive position building in the space processing area with the USSR, West Germany, and Japan emerging as the prime competition for American industry. Japan now makes and sells most of the communications satellite ground stations.

The international situation with respect to space law, on the other hand, is a morass when it comes down to questions of who "owns" the prime locations in geosynchronous Earth orbit, the Moon, or the resources of the planetoid belt. It's in even worse shape when it comes to the SPS. There has been a great deal of high-sounding rhetoric about these things being the "common property of all mankind." This turns out, on close inspection by rational minds, to be a totally null concept. The concepts of ownership, possession, and property are not unique social inventions of the human race. They are common natural traits of most mammals and birds. The concept of property, turf, territory, and possession probably can be traced back to the mammalian and avian instinct to provide for and protect their young, thus insuring species survival. Fish, amphibians, and reptiles don't have the same natural built-in programs. There is no such reality as "common property of all mankind" just as there is no way that either birth or death can be collective realities; each individual can only go through these things or experience these things in his own lonely fashion. The concept of property is individual; young children do not need to be taught this, and they exhibit all the traits of territory, possession, and property in a natural fashion. Lest one believe that human children pick up the territorial trait from their parents, let him carefully observe a litter of puppies.

There is a lot of negotiation, interpretation, and rhetoric going on in space law and international law as it may apply to the space enterprise. A great deal of this is sheer noise being generated by lawyers from the developing Third World nations and from equatorial nations who have suddenly awakened to the facts of the space enterprise. They have grasped the old English common law definition of property—the idea that an individual owns not only the land area of his property, but everything under the land in a wedge down to the center of the Earth and everything outward in an expanding wedge to infinity! Some of this ancient legal lore has been adjudicated in the courts to create the usual legal tangle of earthbound concepts as water rights, mineral rights, right of passage, easements, etc., on and under the land. Individuals no longer control the right of passage of aircraft or spacecraft over their land, but national governments still maintain control of the right of passage of aircraft over their national territory. National governments abrogated their rights to control the passage of spacecraft over their territory on October 4, 1957 when *Sputnik-1* essentially caught every national government and the United States by complete surprise.

Right now, a number of Third World and equatorial

countries are trying to have enough representatives appointed to the U. N. Committee on the Peaceful Uses of Outer Space to give them a majority vote.

The Atillas of the world would like to extend their concept of "permission to pass unmolested" and control by physical force over the space enterprise. Right now, they can't, but they could eventually. The possibility needs to be brought out of the closet so that some action can be taken to prevent the unnecessary extension of national sovereignty beyond the atmosphere because there are some serious military problems involved, as we will see later.

The space enterprise could suffer some major setbacks in such areas as SPS, extraterrestrial materials, and eventual space habitation if improperly negotiated or coordinated treaties were to become a reality.

At the moment, there are no limiting treaties or areas of international law that would seriously limit the space enterprise. While it is true that U.N. treaties to which the United States is a part will not permit you, as an individual, to launch anything into space without the sanctioning of a government, the same holds true if you want to fly an airplane, drive a car, or steer a ship into the territory of another country . . . or even operate within your own nation, for that matter!

But, as the space enterprise becomes more and more successful and as the revenues from space increase because of the growth of space activities, there are going to be those who want a piece of the action without having risked time, money, effort, or lives to make it happen. We are certain to see increased pressure within the United Nations to adopt motions limiting the activities of the space enterprise and attempts to impose taxes, tolls, permits, fees, and other accoutrements of the warlord heritage of national governments. There is probably no way around this, and we will probably have to go through it. The sooner that these political problems are recognized and the sooner the space entrepreneurs move to head them off, the better. It will take plenty of economic and legal planning to avoid serious future problems in this area.

But there will have to be rules, regulations, laws, and treaties. Don't knock politics. It's probably one of the greatest inventions of the human race because it prevents most of us from killing most of the rest of us most of the time. It's only when it fails that it can be criticized. Most politicians are lawyers for the very simple reason that lawyers are highly trained specialists in resolving human conflicts, and politics is the business of resolving conflicts between groups of people. However, it would be a blessing if most of space law could evolve out of terrestrial law *in situ* as the space enterprise progresses and grows. To attempt to write laws in advance of the fact and by second-guessing the development of the technology of the space enterprise—which is something no honest forecaster would ever attempt, but which is occasionally tried by some of the so-called futurists—is highly presumptuous and could restrict or prevent the development of the space enterprise, thwarting its potential for solving a large number of our future problems.

The early years of the space enterprise are the most hazardous in this respect because it does not appear that there will be much of a worldwide market for many of the products and services of the space enterprise at first. The obvious exception to this is the space communications segment which is already in place and which will grow. There is already a proven worldwide market because the majority of the world's basic communications activity today is carried out by means of comsats. This is one area in which considerable international effort should be concentrated in the next 20 years because it can and already has offered a service to the world that the world badly needs: Education.

Herbert George Wells stated in his *Outline of History* in 1920, "Human history becomes more and more a race between education and catastrophe."

The communications satellite—ATS-6 in particular—has amply proved what the space enterprise can accomplish in this regard. The huge comsats, public service communications platforms, and orbital antenna farms of the next decade will make it commonplace to be able to receive television and data directly from the orbiting satellite with very inexpensive and simple ground receiving equipment. This is not hypothetical; it has been done already. From August 1975 to August 1976, ATS-6 transmitted live television broadcasts to inexpensive ground receivers, bringing educational and health information to millions of people in more than 2,500 villages in India. In 1974, more than 600 elementary school teachers in eight Appalachian states participated in graduate-level studies via the ATS-6. Other health and educational programs have been conducted with the ATS-6 in Alaska and the Rocky Mountain states.

The space enterprise can provide the educational system necessary to head off Wells' historical catastrophe.

Space products are another matter. How does a Third World farmer make use of a space product? More important, how does he pay for it? The whole area of space products is still so tenuous that it is very premature to attempt to guess the impact of that segment of the space enterprise on the Third World.

There will obviously be advantages with respect to new biologicals and pharmaceuticals. The World Health Organization believes that smallpox has been eliminated (do they really know about that one isolated tribe or individual in some tropical backwater?). But cholera, dysentery, malaria, and even the plague run rampant through most of the world. Will there be wonder drugs from space to solve these problems? How will they be paid for, and by whom?

Entirely new technologies in the electronics field will probably come from space processing, producing smaller and cheaper solid-state devices that can find real utility in communications and data handling. But what use will a Third World farmer have for a wrist radio? Who does he want to talk to? Who needs to talk to him? Answer these questions, and you've opened the worldwide market. (I could, but somebody else should do some of the work.) Cheaper and better electronic products may mean wider availability of television sets that can receive signals from comsats.

But the extent to which new space materials and products will provide a better and cheaper way for most of the human race to obtain and maintain their basic requirements of food, shelter, clothing, health, and recreation through better tools and materials remains to be worked out.

The basic problems throughout most of the world seem to revolve around people being able to produce enough domestic food to feed themselves rather than planting cash crops for export. Once they are able to do that, they can concentrate on the next step which is to determine and develop their most valuable exportable resource, whether it be raw materials or tourism. Once they have a valuable export, they can pay for the products and services of the space enterprise.

To do this, many nations are going to need energy. The Solar Power Satellite may be one of our most important international products and may turn the United States into an energy exporter within 50 years. But using an SPS that is either owned by the nation or by a private firm based in that nation, or whose output is leased and dedicated to that nation by the SPS owner and operator, is not the straightforward matter that it might appear to be at first.

Nations that already have an electric utility power grid of transmission facilities in place will be the initial customers for an SPS . . . provided they have the available land area for the ground rectenna. The sale of an SPS or its output to such a nation or group of nations is a rather straightforward marketing and sales job. The SPS beam is received at the rectenna and converted to whatever electrical transmission standard is used locally.

But what do you do with a nation that does not have an established electric transmission grid? Can such a nation use the services of an SPS? Yes, if some thought is put into the national requirements and available systems first.

One of the best examples of systems thinking in this area was done by one of the finest experts in world dynamics, Dr. J. Peter Vajk, author of the book, *Doomsday Has Been Cancelled* (Peace Press, Culver City, CA 90230,1978,ISBN 0-915238-24-1). Dr. Vajk's work is one of the best rejoinders to the famous limits to growth concept. It goes as follows, and should be considered only as one example:

India is a subcontinent with a general climate and enough arable land to be able to feed its own people. However, the land is being denuded of trees for firewood, causing erosion and destruction of the land and making it useless for farming. In addition, much of the productive land cannot grow enough food per hectare due to lack of fertilizer. Abundant supplies of excellent fertilizer exist from the cattle in India, but this is not used as fertilizer; it is dried and used as home heating and cooking fuel. This is true throughout most of the Third World.

Use of the output of one or more SPS units by India poses other problems because India does not possess an electric power grid that could distribute the SPS energy to the remote agricultural villages where it might be used for home heating and cooking. India has no Rural Electrification Agency. But India does possess an extensive rail and road transportation system.

If you could put the SPS electricity into a jug and ship it to the hinterlands, you'd have the answer.

You can do it.

Near the rectenna sites, build chemical plants to make methyl alcohol (methanol) from water, air and garbage, using the electricity from the nearby SPS rectenna. It is possible to erect and maintain the rectenna using unskilled labor, since it can be built with prefab aluminum parts, plus imported semiconductor devices. A rectenna is a bolt-together affair. Building the chemical plant will create an expertise in industrial engineering and construction.

While you are doing this, you will have to build up a jug manufacturing capability. You can make the millions of jugs required by using ancient glassblowing methods; you can switch to automated jug manufacture later unless you want to continue to provide employment for glassblowers. Each methanol factory is going to require about two million 8-liter jugs annually. Glass is cheap; it can be made from sand with the energy from the SPS rectenna. If you don't have enough sand, use clay to make ceramic jugs instead. The technology of containers is very old technology and is well-understood and widely practiced throughout the world.

Now throw the switch, the SPS electricity from the rectenna begins producing the methanol, which is put into jugs. Now you've got to distribute these jugs out to the boondocks. Initially, you can use the existing transportation system: railways in the initial distribution phase, then oxcart, handcart, and even bicycle. As your program progresses, you may even want to construct methanol pipelines to regional distribution points, making the pipe from glass or ceramic and using the very large manual labor force of India to install the pipelines. This then permits you to develop an indigenous pipeline technology and expertise, which you can then export along with your expertise in building and operating the methanol plants.

The methanol is delivered to the rural villages in India where it is used for home heating and cooking in methanol stoves which are inexpensive and easy to manufacture, thereby creating another industrial technology.

The use of methanol for home heating and cooking frees up the abundant supply of dung for use as fertilizer, which reduces the foreign exchange imbalance due to present imports of fertilizers. It also improves the ability of the soil to produce higher crop yields, providing India with the capability to eventually feed its own people. If carried far enough, it could make India an *exporter* of agricultural products.

The use of methanol also eliminates the use of more than a billion tons of firewood per year, permitting India to embark upon a program of soil conservation and restoration to increase its arable lands and to reduce erosion.

The extent of this program can be inferred from the fact that India presently uses 20% of its annual biomass production for domestic heating and cooking.

It would require 75 SPS units of 10 gigawatts capacity each to completely fulfill India's electrical requirements by the year 2000. If India embarks upon an SPS utilization program such as the one outlined, the result will be a food self-sufficiency for India plus an export capability for food, methanol factories, pipelines, and methanol heating and cooking stoves. This then puts India in a position to begin paying back the loans obtained to purchase the SPS system or the output of the SPS system.

This also means that if the United States develops the technology and capability to build an SPS system, it can sell either SPS systems or SPS energy internationally, becoming an energy exporter.

When it comes to the international markets for and implications of extraterrestrial materials, we've got to look further down the line into the emerging system of the space enterprise. Initially, there will be a very limited market among Third World nations for ET materials. Raw materials are probably the only exportable resource that most of them possess! Therefore, ET materials may be direct competition. We must remember one thing: Most of us have a very parochial view of the world. Most nations are not worried about environmentalism or conservation; they *want* to exploit their lands in any way that they can regardless of the immediate ecological consequences because they have no other immediate recourse. Food or raw materials are all that they have to sell to pay for the imports that they need to glue their cultures together. The only answer to the dilemma is to so reduce the costs of ET materials and products and services that Third World nations can afford to pay for them through export of their own unique natural resources or services.

At this point, we cannot consider the space enterprise all by itself as an isolated activity of the high-tech nations. Within a quarter of a century, it begins to have major impacts on the entire world just as its communications segment already has.

The world is a system—a complex system. We don't even have an adequate computer model of it yet, regardless of the work of Forester and Meadows at MIT. The space enterprise is a new element in this system, one that has not existed before. It amounts to opening up the closed system of planet Earth, and it is going to cause changes. Whether or not the world is ready for these changes, they are coming. There will be dislocations and problems. The best that we can do is to try to anticipate some of these and soften them as much as possible.

The alternative to the space enterprise, is much worse.

CHAPTER TEN

The world still has far too many men on horseback. Too many Atillas. Too many people who still operate on the social philosophy of a world of scarcity: If you don't have it, you take it away from somebody who does. In the days before the industrial revolutions created a situation of abundance in the industrial cultures, some people discovered that it was relatively easy in a world of scarcity to take things from other people through the use of physical force. And if you didn't need it, you could force them to pay you to keep you from taking it, even though you didn't want it. You could easily run a protection racket which included the ability to collect tolls and other fees to guarantee a traveler or merchant safe passage through lands that you controlled by force. You could charge others a fee or a tax for using something you controlled by force.

Atilla's progeny still control most of the world.

And if you don't like Atilla and what he and his cohorts could do to you, you'd better be prepared to meet him with similar or overwhelming means of physical force of your own.

To a merchant or entrepreneur, this is ridiculous and a waste of precious time and effort, goods, materials, and people. The entrepreneur works on a different philosophy, the industrial philosophy that has emerged only during the past two centuries: If you don't have what you want or need, you make it instead of take it. Don't create slaves, serfs, and subjugated populations; create and serve customers instead because it is easier and more efficient.

Efficiency is going to win out in the long run because of the biological Law of Least Effort.

But in the meantime, we are going to have to be prepared to use physical force to hold on to what we have created in the space enterprise and to prevent its use by the Atillas of the world for their own ends . . . which are not compatible with the goals of the space enterprise.

All of which boils down to the simple fact that there are military implications to the space enterprise and that we'd better face this reality right from the start and be prepared.

There are going to be conflicts between owners of comsats because of crowding in the preferred positions of geosynchronous orbit, because of the frequency allocations, because of interference problems, and because of the fact that the high power output made possible by complexity inversion is going to permit anybody with a three-foot dish antenna made from chicken wire to pick up any television program beamed in his direction. Electronics technology is now well past the point of no return; it takes very little to obtain a needed transistor or LSI chip of the kind you really need, and the know-how to put these things together to make receivers is becoming more and more widespread. Atilla doesn't like his people to receive any communications other than what he transmits. He wants to educate them and inform them *his way*. If he gets into a disagreement with somebody else and it escalates into an armed conflict, the first thing he is going to have to do is to knock out his opponent's communications, data handling, and surveillance. Which means he's going to have to seize, destroy, or disable some satellites.

Communications satellites, data handling satellites, Earth resources satellites, weather satellites, and other communications service space systems of the space enterprise are going to have to be protected against military force.

A space manufacturing facility producing a product of great value, even something as prosaic as space jewelry, is going to have to have the same protection against seizure or destruction as any industrial plant on Earth. Somebody is either going to take it to have its output for himself, or he's going to destroy it because it creates competition for *his* products. This is especially true of any space manufacturing facility that happens to produce anything that makes a future weapons system possible . . . and this can be any number of otherwise commonplace industrial products. People still remember Schweinfurt, Germany; the United States expended a lot of B-17 bombers and their crews trying to knock out the production of little ball bearings at Schweinfurt. Tanks, guns, trucks, and airplanes don't run well if they don't have ball bearings. There will be comparable situations with regard to space manufacturing facilities in the event of future warfare.

But, in warfare, if you can manage to knock out an energy supply, it's much more effective. Flattening the Schweinfurt ball bearing plants wasn't nearly as effective as attacking and destroying the German energy sources—the hydroelectric plants of the Rhur dams, the Ploesti oil refineries, and the petrol storage facilities. Germany still had tanks and airplanes ready to go on VE Day in 1945, but there was no fuel to make them go.

An SPS is going to be a big, fat, juicy target. If you can't manage to knock it out of action, maybe you can take it over and redirect the energy beam to your *own* simple and cheaply made rectenna system. Or redirect the beam to your own space-based weapons systems to power them.

There has been some talk about the capabilities of an SPS as a weapon itself. Some people have speculated on the possibility of using the microwave beam as a weapon, literally frying cities like a super microwave oven. Or using laser-beamed power to burn things to the ground. First of all, an SPS can be designed with these possibilities in mind so that it is not possible without severe and very costly modifications to focus the microwave beam or the laser beam into a pencil of energy with enough energy density to do these dastardly things. A mere 23 milliwatts per square centimeter in a microwave beam won't boil any water. And it can be stopped entirely by a sheet of aluminum foil. The same logic holds for laser beaming. And at high energy densities, such beams run into trouble with atmospheric dispersion. It would indeed be nice if we had access to some of the highly classified military data on high-power lasers; it might eliminate some of the general ignorance in this whole energy beam area and therefore dispel some of the fear that accompanies ignorance. One thing is certain: What happens in a home microwave oven or in an industrial welding laser isn't within several orders of magnitude of what we are talking about when it comes to SPS energy beams.

As a weapon, the SPS as presently envisioned is not

going to have enough effect to make it worthwhile to expend the money, time and effort to utilize it for destructive purposes. There will be much more effective weapons systems that have been developed on Earth for use against Earth targets and totally new weapons systems based in space itself as a consequence of the development of space technology in the space enterprise.

There is no way that we can stop the technology of the space enterprise being used for military purposes any more than we can proceed with the space enterprise without considering the military implications. Technology is what you make of it. As long as there are Atillas in the world, one had best be prepared to handle them with the only thing they understand: physical force.

In addition, the space enterprise involves taking more than industrial operations into space. It means taking along parts of our highly evolved cultural heritages and social organizations to forestall disagreements and to resolve conflicts. These are the rules, codes, regulations, laws and treaties that we have individually and collectively agreed to observe. But they are effective only when the majority of people involved abide by them and when you've got some way to enforce compliance.

This means both military and police organizations, and there is a fine line of distinction between them. In our culture, the police organization handles internal compliance while the military organization takes care of the protection of people and property external to the national boundaries. In some cultures, there is no difference whatsoever between the police and the military organizations.

We're certainly going to discover that the space enterprise will have the equivalent of today's current industrial security activities that surround Earth-based industry with a quiet and unobtrusive barrier: the security guards and the company cops. These are usually very effective. It's often easier to get into a classified military base than to gain entry into a factory. Industrial security is many times more stringent than military security.

Brinks, Wells Fargo, and Purolator are going to have their counterparts in the space enterprise. Firms engaged in the space enterprise may find it cheaper and easier to hire security firms than to set up their own security force, just as they do on Earth. Most companies would much rather be guarded by Pinkertons than by the Marines. This sort of paramilitary force in space doesn't face the same problems and potential as a purely military force; they are the police force. They also represent another aspect of the space enterprise that few people think about when they first consider doing things out there.

The technology of the space enterprise is going to present the police-military organizations not only with new technologies but with new doctrines, rationales, and operational realities. This is because the zone of police-military operations will be in space which is not only three-dimensional but also governed by the energy realities of the gravity wells we spoke of earlier. This was recognized as long ago as 1960 by the late pioneer futurist and space planner, Dandridge M. Cole, who formulated his "Panama Theory" of the military implications of space. This can be briefly stated:

"There are strategic areas in space—vital to future scientific, military, and commercial space programs—which could be excluded from our use through occupation and control by unfriendly powers.

This statement is based on the assumption that in colonizing space, man (and other intelligent beings) will compete for the more desirable areas."

When this is applied just to military space operations in the Earth-Moon system, the prime strategic doctrine is that of the gravity well, which requires that one be at the top of a gravity well or, at least, higher up in a gravity well than his adversary. The military analogy to this doctrine is the proven doctrine of the high ground. During the age of sailing ships in the world's ocean navies, it was a matter of getting upwind of your opponent, using the "wind gauge."

The important feature of the gravity well is that it provides an exceptional energy advantage and a maneuvering advantage to the person on the high ground. It takes far less energy to maneuver high in a gravity well or in a shallower gravity well. This gives you better flexibility and more capability for maneuvering.

A simple analogy demonstrates this concept. Put one person at the bottom of a well and another at the top of the well. Give them both rocks to throw at each other. Who's going to get hurt worse? Who's going to have more time to see the other's rocks coming and be able to maneuver out of the way? Who's going to have more opportunity to do something about the oncoming rocks? And whose rock will have more energy when it reaches its target?

The man at the top of the well possesses an obvious and classical military advantage.

The logical consequence of this gravity well doctrine leads inevitably to the most important military fact of the space enterprise: Military control of the Moon means military control of the Earth. And military control of either the L4 or L5 lunar libration points (60 degrees ahead and behind the Moon in its orbit) means control of the entire Earth-Moon system. Since the Earth-Moon system is going to be the center of the action of the space enterprise for at least a century, this means that whoever controls the places where Dr. O'Neill wants to put space colonies will also be able to control the Earth-Moon system, a goal that is far beyond anything ever attempted or accomplished by Alexander the Great, the Roman emperors, Ghengis Khan, the Moslem Caliphs, Napoleon, or Adolph Hitler.

Control means that you are able to impose your will upon the flow of space-going commerce, to protect your own facilities in space, to deny the use of other military and/or commercial orbital areas to others, to launch strikes against *any* target on the surface of either the Earth or the Moon or against anything in any orbit, and to detect and take action against any potential threat before the weapon reaches you. This is not to say that I am encouraging this nor even advocating it; I am merely pointing out the logical military consequences of the purely peaceful commercial uses of space. To ignore them is to place the entire space enterprise in jeopardy. To plan for them and to take various space weapons systems into consideration is like buying an accident insurance policy; one sincerely hopes one never will have to make a claim against it.

What possible weapons can we anticipate being used in military space operations? To get an answer to that, we've got to look first at the basic concept of a weapon. A weapon doesn't have to have a physical reality and it doesn't have to be used to be effective; an opponent must believe that the weapon exists and that you will use it. Basically, weapons fall into the following general categories:

Mass manipulators: These produce physical damage by using the basic inertial characteristics of matter and the conversion of potential energy (the energy of position) to kinetic energy (energy resulting from motion). Such weapons systems include subclasses of mass projectors, penetration weapons, mass detectors, and decoys.

Energy manipulators: These weapons produce physical damage by the application of large quantities of energy in a very short period of time in a limited volume. Explosives are one example. In addition to the subclasses of the mass manipulators, we can add the subclass of energy concentrators to this area.

Biological manipulators: These are weapons that produce damage to organic life forms or other chemicals. We've lived with them for years on Earth. They include poison gases, nerve gases, disease vectors, and disease agents themselves.

Psychological manipulators: Everyone thinks that psychological weapons are new, but they rank among the oldest. They change the mental condition of the opponent so that his will or capability to resist is diminished or eliminated. Among the actual weapons of this class are propaganda, counterintelligence, brainwashing, covert manipulation of the information media, mood-altering drugs, consciousness-altering drugs, and mind-altering drugs.

Some weapons systems are a combination of one or more of these basic classifications. Some require a vehicle to transport them to the point of use or application.

Every weapon or weapon system that you can think of falls into these four basic classifications. The specific design of a weapon and how it is used depends upon where you have to use it.

This isn't academic. We're trying to get a real handle on possible space weapons. Until we do, we don't know what to defend against. Or how to defend against it. Or whether it can be countered at all. The space environment permits an unusual array of weapons to be developed and used . . . and it likewise renders some very obvious weapons quite useless and ineffective.

Even for purposes of the industrial side of the space enterprise, it would help if we could categorize the various regions of the Earth-Moon system all by itself. The Solar System is a different matter entirely.

The various regions of space in the Earth-Moon system are nothing more than specific zones within the gravity wells of the system. We can consider them to be a series of spheres, some with Earth as their centers, others with specific celestial bodies such as the Moon at their centers, and some with no real centers at all, just locational points. In a sense, these resemble the energy levels of electrons around an atomic nucleus.

Near-Earth Orbit (NEO) extends from an arbitrary defined level of 50 miles above the Earth's surface to approximately 200 miles up, well below most of the radiation of the Van Allen Belts.

Cislunar Space (CLS) extends from 200 miles from the Earth out to the orbit of the Moon *except* that region around the Moon where the lunar gravity well predominates over the gravity wells of the Earth and the Sun. It includes the geosynchronous orbit 22,200 miles above the Earth.

Lunar Surface Orbit (LSO) includes both lunar orbits within the lunar gravity well and the surface of the Moon, which is also a military operational region.

Translunar Space (TLS) extends from the lunar orbit out to a distance where the gravity well of the Sun pre-

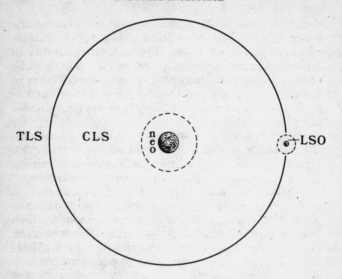

dominates over the gravity wells of the Earth and the Moon. This is roughly a half-million miles from the surface of the Earth.

Beyond TLS there is *Solar System Space (SSS)* which is dominated by the gravity well of the Sun in which all the planets orbit. The solar gravity well is dimpled here and there by the moving gravity wells of the various planets.

In each of these operational space areas, there are unique considerations that affect military doctrine, tactical operations, and weapons systems.

NEO is a valuable military area for Earth-launched and Earth-oriented activities. It is already being used this way, and it can easily be reached quickly from the Earth's surface by any space vehicle capable of attaining about 26,000 feet per second velocity. In the 1970 decade, at least six nations are conducting reconnaissance and surveillance operations in NEO. At least two nations possess manned spacecraft capability in NEO. In the era of the space enterprise, NEO will be useful for quick–look and high-detail surveillance of both Earth-based targets and space facilities; for satellite hunter-killer operations if you want to disable an opponent's NEO space system; as a staging area for manned surface-to-surface troop strike transports using the space transportation technology of the space enterprise; and for "quick-dip" hypersonic skimming of the upper atmosphere by manned or unmanned craft for surveillance, recon, or offensive activity.

Thus, NEO is basically a tactical area for Earth-centered operations. It is also the region through which Earth-based ICBMs must pass during most of their flight, and it is therefore the region in which ICBMs are most vulnerable to being intercepted by other missiles or by energy beam weapons in space.

In spite of the fact that NEO is reasonably far up on the side of the Earth gravity well in terms of the energy you need to reach the region from the surface, even today's technology permits the use of rapid-ascent satellite interceptors. For this reason, NEO is a region where you've got an alarming lack of capability to respond to attack because you don't have much time to react.

There has been a lot of talk, discussion, and fear-mongering about a manned military space station in NEO. Forget it. It's a very large target traveling in a predictable path. In the opening moments of any conflict where its presence would be a factor, it can be disabled by satellite hunter-killers or beam weapons. (Why wasn't some sort of satellite interceptor used against *Skylab*? Simply because it would have merely broken up *Skylab* into many pieces that would have had a much larger landing footprint.)

Cislunar Space (CLS) is another matter. It's a valuable zone of maneuver and recon because it is further up the sides of the Earth's gravity well. Therefore, even though more energy is required to get into CLS, less energy is required to maneuver in it. It is also the region that includes geosynchronous orbit where a satellite will stay over one spot on the Earth because the orbital period is 24 hours. Geosynch is already crowded with several hundred satellites for surveillance, navigation, communications, data transfer, weather monitoring, and information gathering in general. In the 1990s, it will be the region occupied by the SPS system.

CLS is much more secure against Earth-launched or even NEO–launched threats because of the time required for vehicles to climb up the sides of the gravity well to this region. The primary importance of CLS is the location and characteristics of the lunar libration points, which we'll talk more about shortly.

LSO has quite different characteristics. Because of the mass of the Moon, the prime location for a military base is probably below the lunar surface. It is the prime location for one of the most important space weapons systems we can forecast, a weapon system and a weapon itself that is very old. The weapon system is the lunar surface catapult, sometimes referred to as a mass driver. It doesn't make any difference what you call it; it is a rock-thrower. The Moon is the best site in the Earth–Moon system for this weapon because there are a lot of Moon rocks around to throw—a very large ammunition supply. The Moon provides a very stable base that will increase accuracy. And there is ample solar energy available for power.

You could put a smaller mass driver in the weightlessness of space, but when you launch something from there at very high speed you've got to be very careful that the reaction forces don't misalign your unit for the next shot.

The lunar catapult or mass driver is a critical system for the space enterprise. It can also be used as a formidable weapon.

A large lunar catapult capable of hurling a one-ton load into space can be quickly converted into a Earth bombardment system. It is non-nuclear. It is not governed by any existing UN treaties. And it can be very effective. The Barringer Meteor Crater in Arizona was created by the impact of an 80-foot diameter nickel-iron meteorite weighing a little more than 1,000 tons, and the impact was roughly equivalent to a 2.5-megaton bomb with no nuclear effects. A one-ton rock hitting the Earth at seven miles per second releases the energy equivalent of more than 14 tons of TNT, equivalent to a 28,800-ton bomb. The biggest bomb dropped by the Allies on Germany during World War II was the 22,000-pound "Grand Slam" blockbuster. If you can throw a hundred-ton load with a lunar catapult, the impact energy release would be equivalent to two kilotons of TNT, the amount of energy released by a small nuclear weapon . . . but without the nuclear side-effects.

Small mass drivers can be used as weapons, too. They could launch small loads in rapid succession like Space Gatling Guns. The impact of a one kilogram mass (2.2 pounds) traveling at several miles per second could do considerable damage to any space facility, especially when several hundred or even thousand such projectiles hit in rapid succession.

No explosives are required for such space weapons. The conversion of kinetic energy based on mass and the square of the velocity is quite sufficient to damage delicate solar power panels, communications antennas, heat radiators, and unprotected pressure hulls of manned ships and stations.

By now, it should be fairly obvious why we cannot ignore the military implications of the space enterprise. Catapults and mass drivers used for commercial purposes must be subjected to some sort of control against their use as military bombardment weapons.

When you get beyond lunar orbit, in TLS, you are in a zone of maneuver and rendezvous for space vehicles with great abilities for velocity changes using their propulsion systems. There is a location in this zone, however, that could be used as a military staging point, the L2 lunar libration point beyond the Moon and in line with the Earth and the Moon.

The drawing indicates the five lunar libration points. A "libration point" is a special solution of the famous "three-body" problem. Two bodies will revolve around one another because of their gravity fields. Three bodies pose another problem because you must consider the interaction of the three gravity fields on the three bodies simultaneously. In a system such as the Earth–Moon system, there are five locations where you could put any other body and where it would be in balance with the gravitational fields. These are known as "libration points." One of them is between the Earth and the Moon. One of them is beyond the Moon. One is on the opposite side of the Earth from the Moon. And there are two libration points in lunar orbit—one 60 degrees behind the Moon, and the

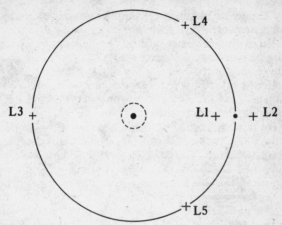

Orbits: The outer circle represents geosynchronous orbit, 23,500 miles from the Earth's surface. The inner, broken, circle represents a near-earth orbit (NEO) at 1,000 miles. Drawing is to scale.

other 60 degrees ahead of the Moon. These latter two points, known as L4 and L5, are the two most stable libration points in the system; the other three are slightly unstable and will require a small amount of energy to put anything located there back into equilibrium from time to time.

The L4 and L5 lunar libration points have been suggested by Dr. Gerard K. O'Neill as the primary locations for both space manufacturing facilities and very large space colonies. However, very few people have recognized the extreme importance of the L4 and L5 locations from a military point of view.

Both L4 and L5 are stable locations within the Earth-Moon system; neither possesses a gravity well; both sit atop the gravity wells of both the Earth and the Moon. Both L4 and L5 sit atop the best hills in the

Military base S2 at the L-5 Lagrangian Point in lunar orbit, a prime military system.

site because it is atop the gravity wells of everything in the Earth-Moon

Earth-Moon system, so to speak. They are the easiest locations to control and the best locations to use for military purposes.

I have been unable to find any discussion of the military implications of the L4 and L5 sites. If the military implications have been considered, they have been classified as a military secret, dismissed as unimportant, or simply ignored.

Their importance lies in the fact that those who have space facilities at L4/L5—or on the Moon, for that matter—can offer no guarantee that they will always be used for peaceful industrial purposes. Authors such as Heinlein and Bova have already speculated about revolutions or grievances that could trigger military actions in space. There are any number of lessons from history where an industrious, hard-working group of close-knit people have taken a sharp turn in their external affairs and become a militant culture.

How can we handle the military implications of the space enterprise? I don't know. I haven't studied them long enough. I can only point out some of the doctrines and call attention to the problem here. It deserves its own book. Maybe someone will write one . . . and *soon*. In this regard, I feel a little like my colleague Herman Kahn who was the first to have the guts to "think about the unthinkable"—to consider the conduct and consequences of thermonuclear war.

It will take the best minds and the most careful diplomacy of the next hundred years to come up with livable solutions to the military implications of the space enterprise.

We cannot ignore the coming reality of the military implications of the space enterprise any more than we can ignore the reality of our everyday lives and disband the local police force. In one way, the space enterprise is no different than our other activities: We must attempt to build a universe of law where matters of human conflict can be solved by judgement, arbitration, or negotiation. The law must always be backed up by the means to enforce the rules, by physical coercion if necessary. This will always be the case as long as Atillas exist among us . . . and that will probably be for a very long time.

CHAPTER ELEVEN

Space is the real utopia of today's generation of young people, who will be the ones who run the world in the 21st Century. The news media have given an inordinate and undeserved amount of exposure and attention to the Neo-Luddites, those modern versions of the organized bands of hoodlums that originally appeared in the English Midlands in 1811, smashing textile machinery because they believed that machinery would eliminate the jobs of weavers. The space utopians hark to different music than the mobs who would turn off technology, shut down the nukes, permanently ground all aircraft as being intrinsically unsafe, and bring the world to what amounts to a thermonuclear standstill (although the Neo-Luddites do not honestly realize that this can be the only logical consequence of success on their part).

The space advocates of today would have us move out of the womb of Mother Earth, to live free in space colonies, and to eventually make the space enterprise happen. In this regard, Dr. Gerald K. O'Neill has been a powerful and moving force in late 20th Century life; by making a synthesis of the work of many others who preceded him, by sensing the tenor of the young people who could not abide a future of terror, scarcity, want, and sacrifice, and by knowing how to present this to the world, O'Neill has truly created a grassroots movement advocating space.

The utopia of the O'Neill generation is hopeful, optimistic, and positive. They are going to live happily ever after in space colonies built from lunar materials at L4 and L5. Life in these space colonies is portrayed as pastoral with grass, trees, farm animals, and clouds drifting in a strange inside-out world.

Everyone in the space colonies will be involved in some sort of business supporting the colonies. The colonists will build and operate space factories and the SPS system.

This is a worthy and plausible dream. *I'm all for it.*

But we've got to get from where we are to where we want to be. We must manage to make it through the next quarter of a century, a most difficult time, in order to establish the space enterprise as a going affair. Then we will be able to build and live in these space habitats.

The O'Neill space colonies, space habitats, or space settlements will indeed come to pass . . . or something like them, at any rate. But only as a *consequence* of the space enterprise, and not the other way around.

Between Space Shuttle and the space colony, there is a *tremendous* amount of work to be done. It must be done, and it will be done. It will be very risky; there will be millions of dollars invested and perhaps thousands of lives lost. It will be very expensive. It will be hard work.

People on Earth are likely to be living a utopian pastoral existence long before it is achieved in space.

Living in space is going to be hard, deadly, uncomfortable, and restrictive . . . for a long time. Every frontier has been this way, and there is no reason to believe that the high frontier is going to be any different.

A confirmed space utopian will have stopped reading by now. So the rest of us who are ready and willing to pioneer a new frontier can proceed.

The concept of the space enterprise is, after all, a "monstrous plot." It's a scheme to get people to leave the womb of Mother Earth, to expand outward into the Universe, to begin what Heinlein has termed "the Great Diaspora." The whole reason for doing *anything* off-planet is because human beings are or will someday be there. It's exciting to watch the pictures from *Viking* on Mars or *Voyager* swinging around Jupiter. It's also extremely frustrating because it's only a *machine* out there making those pictures; there is no human there experiencing the whole activity. There is a considerable difference between watching the pictures from a remote, unmanned probe and watching the TV picture of people living and working in space and on the surface of the Moon. We've done all of this up to now for exploration, and it has wearied many people because it is something that only a few can participate in directly. What we needed was a way for many people to participate. More important, we needed a way to appeal to their self-interest. We had to show that it would be possible to make a buck out there.

This economic factor is a powerful driver. Since The Third Industrial Revolution was initially proposed even as the last Apollo astronauts were walking on the Moon in 1972, we have witnessed an upsurge of awakening among people toward recognition of what this really all means.

The key to creating a frontier isn't just for the sake

of exploration alone; there has always been an economic factor and a means for people to get involved.

So the space enterprise isn't just a matter of comsats, space products, SPS, extraterrestrial materials, economics, transportation, military implications, and the rest. All of these things intimately involve *people* who will design them, pay for them, build them, operate them, repair them, and cause it all to happen.

The exciting thing about the NASA Space Shuttle is *not* that it is mostly reusable, nor that it can orbit such large payloads, nor that it can do so on a regular weekly schedule. The important thing about the NASA Space Shuttle is the fact that it will be able to do all of these things with up to *seven people* aboard each time! Since we have been involved up to now with putting only three people in space at one time on an irregular basis, *this* is what makes the Space Shuttle important.

Ordinary people able to pass the equivalent of the Third Class Medical exam of the Federal Aviation Administration (which is about as exclusive as a rainstorm; if you cast a shadow, that's about 50% of the requirement) will be able to fly into orbit in Space Shuttle after about six weeks of training. For the first time ever, space will not be the exclusive domain of a few highly trained, physically perfect jet fighter pilots. To fly the ships of space for some time to come, until we have space pilots who were born in space and therefore fully conditioned to a three–dimensional weightless universe, space pilots will be highly trained and experienced jet pilots. But the people who work in space can be and will be anybody and everybody willing and able to go.

The progress of people in space appears to be straightforward right now.

The first few years of Space Shuttle operations will

see more than a hundred people—scientists, industrial researchers, even TV personalities—traveling into near–Earth orbit and back as crewmembers aboard the Shuttle. (The Shuttle has not been certified as a passenger-carrying aircraft by the FAA because of an agreement between NASA and FAA; therefore, the Shuttle cannot carry passengers, only "crewmembers.") They will be true pioneers, the first to follow in the footsteps of astronauts. They will be the first space people.

There are already plans afoot to turn *SpaceLab* into a free–flying module. With the addition of a power pack to supply solar-generated electricity and to radiate waste heat away from the module, the free-flying *SpaceLab* can be left in orbit, manned, for more than a month. At first, this free-flying *SpaceLab* will be recovered from orbit by a Shuttle and brought back to Earth for refurbishment. Eventually, within a few years as the technology matures, *SpaceLab* will be put into orbit and used by several crews who are brought up by Shuttle; *SpaceLab* will be refurbished in space with new supplies by the Shuttle.

The Soviets are already doing this and are therefore at least five years ahead of us when it comes to permanent manned space facilities that can be refurbished in orbit. *Salyut-6* has served as home to six cosmonauts for long-duration stays; nine *Soyuz* spacecraft have brought men and materials to *Salyut-6*. And *Salyut-6* has been resupplied with rocket propellants for orbital station-keeping, oxygen, food, and scientific materials by six *Progress* unmanned cargo space ships. The Soviet Union has quietly slipped into Number One position in space again after the disastrous years of 1964–1972 when the United States was so patently ahead in space technology.

"But we beat them to the Moon, didn't we? So who cares?" This is the current reaction of most Americans—except those of us who know that we are engaged today in a much different competition than going to the Moon for exploration purposes. The Soviets are now in orbit doing research on space processing that Americans will not be able to do for several years; plus the fact that the Soviet Union has in hand a workable system for continuous manned operations in space.

So, in talking about people in space, we're going to have to confine the discussion to what free world people can do if they want to; we have no inside track on Soviet planning except that we know that it will be an economic race.

The next step beyond the free–flying *SpaceLab* module amounts to a "space camp." It involves the use of the External Tank of the Space Shuttle as a rudimentary large-volume space station capable of being outfitted in space by Shuttles for long-duration habitation such as the Soviets are now doing with *Salyut*. Instead of permitting only two or three people to live in space aboard the free–flying *SpaceLab*, the rudimentary "space industrial park" made up initially of a single External Tank could be inhabited by six to ten people at once. This "space industrial park" will grow by accretion as additional External Tanks are put into orbit (one is used for each Shuttle flight) until there are several linked together. As early as 1985 this could serve two purposes: (a) to support the increasing amount of space processing of materials and products, and (b) to permit the conduct of experiments moving toward the pilot plant SPS unit with a 1987 deadline for the go/no-go decision point. We've made the assumption that there will be one, if not several, new products that derive from the first five years of research and development in the space environment aboard *SpaceLab* and from some of the early Getaway Specials. (This is like visiting a circus or a zoo; you know that "there's gotta be an elephant in there somewhere.")

This Space Industrial Park will probably be placed in a low–Earth orbit to make it very easy to reach with Shuttle on a regular basis. In fact, ease of access to the park may take mission preference over the ability of the Shuttle to loft its maximum payload; some payload may be off-loaded to enable the Shuttle to fly a

An early space industrial park in near-Earth orbit about 1995. It is made up of hexagonal factory modules clustered along a central spine and looks like it has just grown almost randomly in common with most industrial plants on Earth. It is surrounded by a considerable amount of sky junk.

"dog-leg" maneuver to get into a true equatorial Space Industrial Park orbit, for example. Or the Shuttle may be uprated with additional boosters (now contemplated) or with more efficient boosters (now in the planning and study stage).

In fact, if space processing is successful far beyond our grandest dreams (and this is more likely than a complete failure), there may be more than one space industrial park. Depending upon the degree of activity in space processing, these rudimentary space stations built up on an opportunistic basis (as is nearly every factory on Earth) would be inhabited by up to 50 people. Some would be running space processing operations. Others would be monitoring and refurbishing remote space processing operations that are taking place in nearby free–flying manufacturing modules because the process may be far too hazardous to permit its conduct in the park complex itself. This could be true of biological products, for example, where it would be more than a slight nuisance to have a virus get loose. Space manufacturing offers the very best opportunity available for conducting industrial operations and processes in complete and total isolation.

Other inhabitants of the Park would be involved in housekeeping operations, although there would be a strong effort made to keep these tasks as automatic as possible. Yet, when you've got a very large operation going, you've got to have a janitor. Some things like stopped-up plumbing just won't take care of themselves. And since the Park is probably going to grow like Topsy, in spite of the wails and teeth–gnashing of some space planners who would like to see nice, well-organized and well-planned space facilities of the type depicted by aerospace company artists, I'm willing to

bet they can't maintain this aseptic appearance and
operation by 1990—unless the whole space enterprise
has become a big government operation in which
cleanliness is next to Godliness. In domestic industry,
cleanliness is next to impossible except where it
counts, which is usually in an industrial process where
dirt can't be tolerated. ("Dirt" has lots of definitions;
in industry, it is any material in the process or product
that you don't *want* in the process or product. Probably the world's greatest dirt experts work for Eastman
Kodak where dirt is something that you've *got* to keep
out of the process for making and developing photo-
graphic film!)

Space products being manufactured in Space Industrial Parks can, by the year 1990, result in several
hundred if not a thousand people living in space for
periods of several months at a time. Transportation
costs are still going to be high, and it is going to be
more economical—weightless pathology permitting—to put people in orbit and supply them
for as long as physiologically and psychologically feasible.

If a positive decision on SPS is made by 1987, the
number of people in space can increase drastically by
several orders of magnitude in the 1990 decade.

A commitment to a pilot plant SPS means the availability of the Heavy–Lift Launch Vehicle derived from
the Space Shuttle, plus the possible conversion of the
manned Shuttle to carry up to 74 people per launch in
a special module inserted into the payload bay. Somebody is going to have to be up there to put the pilot
plant together, the space-going equivalent of today's
"high steel men" who bolt together high-rise buildings and skyscrapers. But they will be operating fantastic machines known as beam–builders that will

fabricate structural members in space from raw materials. Grumman Aerospace has already built and demonstrated a beam–builder for aluminum beams and girders, but it is quite likely that most of the space structures will be fabricated in orbit by beam machines using advanced composite plastic materials that offer a better strength-to-weight ratio. After all, when it costs about $300 for every pound you take into orbit, you do the job with the lightest material you can find!

Initially, there will be only a few dozen people at a time involved in constructing the SPS pilot plant. Once it is on line and working, there will be only a few people—less than a dozen—working out all the little problems, glitches, and bugs that are present in the design and construction of *any* new device.

In some ways the construction and operation of the pilot plant SPS will resemble an analogous activity on Earth: the construction and operation of an offshore oil rig. A few people live on these rigs, and they are supplied from time to time by helicopter or supply boat. It's comfortable, but it is also lonely and can be very dangerous. The pilot plant is going to be much smaller than a full-sized SPS—perhaps only one gigawatt in output. But handling even a billion watts of electricity in space can be hazardous when the most handled up to that point is perhaps several hundred kilowatts for the Space Industrial Parks. It's going to be a real job learning how to build and operate an SPS, and the task of doing it with the pilot plant is going to be doubly difficult because, hopefully, all the mistakes are going to be made with the pilot plant. Some of these mistakes are going to be deadly. But, with careful but not overly cautious design, these can be minimized. They can never be totally eliminated, even when engineers study it to death ahead of time. In fact, such over-study actually has a tendency to make things much more dangerous because it is very difficult to stop playing the game of "what would happen if?" and to quit putting safety devices on the safety devices. Probably the biggest job of field engineers today is taking off or otherwise disabling the safety devices that were insisted upon by some home-office engineer who never had to make it work on site . . .

Unless some totally unsuspected problem comes up, one that has been completely overlooked by everyone who has considered the SPS system to date, the pilot plant SPS is going to show us how to build and operate the total SPS system including an evaluation of the biological and ecological effects around the rectennas on the ground. With a commitment to an SPS system in the 1989–1991 time period, the entire space enterprise begins to move rapidly. Even if SPS is not feasible, we will have available by 1990 a Shuttle-derived Heavy–Lift Launch Vehicle, plus two unmanned upper stages to boost equipment into geosynchronous orbit, plus at least one manned orbital transfer vehicle capable of lifting people to geosynchronous orbit to work on communications satellites and public service platforms. Also, by 1990, we must have a replacement for the current NASA Space Shuttle for one simple reason: The Space Shuttles will be nearing the end of their designed useful lifetimes. Intended originally for only 50 flights, this has now been extended to 100 flights; one flight per week over a ten-year period with the four orbiters currently planned and funded means that we will have simply worn them out. We'll probably have more than four Space Shuttle orbiters, and it would not surprise me if there were as many as ten operational Orbiters by 1990. But, by that time, the current Space Shuttle technology will be obsolete. There will be new materials, new equipment, and new operational techniques. If we have done our homework properly and turned the Space Shuttle operations over to a private firm, NASA will have developed the Shuttle's replacement.

A single-stage-to-orbit space transportation vehicle to follow Shuttle is not only feasible with 1980 technology or technology that we know is coming, but it is inevitable because of the design life of the Space Shuttle of today.

If we embark upon an SPS construction program of building at least two 10-gigawatt SPS units per year, and if we start out (as we must) by bringing up all materials from Earth, we've got to build a LEO staging base plus a construction base in geosynchronous orbit. The LEO base is simply a pass-through operation where payloads are transferred from HLLV Big Onions to Cargo Orbital Transfer Vehicles (COTV) and where people are transferred from personnel launch vehicles to personnel orbital transfer vehicles for the flight out to geosynch. Fleet size requirements are four HLLV Big Onions plus the five Space Shuttle Orbiters—or six Big Onions; two personnel shuttles to carry people up to LEO; 23 COTV ships; and two Personnel Orbital Transfer Vehicles.

It is going to require about 35 people to operate the LEO staging base. And there will be approximately 700 people required at the construction base in geosynchronous orbit. Plus about 100 people to operate the transportation system and space ship fleet. NASA has estimated these numbers on the basis of permitting an SPS worker to remain in space for a 90-day period before returning to Earth for R & R, and each worker putting in an eight-hour day and a six-day week in orbit. So, each year, we've got 835 people in space building two 10-gigawatt SPS units.

This in itself is quite a housekeeping program and is probably very conservative in estimating the numbers of people required. It would not be surprising if there were at least 1,000 people involved in space in the SPS program, plus another couple of thousand on R & R on Earth, plus thousands of others on Earth getting payloads ready to loft into space. There will be thousands more involved in building the rectennas on Earth.

This is going to go on for at least a quarter of a century as we build more and more SPS units to supply more electricity to Earth and eventually to take over more and more of the electrical baseload.

Of course, these numbers get shot down completely when we begin to talk about using extraterrestrial materials for building SPS units in the year 2000 and after. The numbers go up rapidly, but the cost comes down just as rapidly. Once that basic space transportation system capable of hauling large numbers of people and heavy payloads up from Earth is in place and operating, costs for space transportation not only begin to come down rapidly but the state of the art of space technology will permit us to build and operate many new and different types of space vehicles with a lower cost.

The space enterprise is, after all, a positive feedback system that, once started, grows because of itself.

By the year 2000, after a decade of SPS construction, and almost two decades of successful space processing and product manufacture, we're talking about thousands of people in space, living off–planet for months at a time, some never wanting to go back "home" to Earth. A lot of people who built the Trans Alaska pipe-

line elected to stay in Alaska. And people who built our
railroads in the last century elected to stay in places
they thought they liked better. Will space be any different?

At the turn of the century, we are no longer talking
about the cramped and primitive living quarters and
conditions of the free–flying modules, the external
tanks cobbled together into the initial Space Industrial Parks, or the early space camps resembling off-
shore oil rig living. Even with the SPS construction
base in geosynchronous orbit, where more than 800
people will be living at a time, we are talking about
early space settlements.

We'll learn a number of new things in the exciting
decades of the 1990s and 2000s.

We'll learn exactly how to build those closed-cycle
life support systems we need for exploiting the Moon
and the planetoid belt with long flights and long-duration stays in space. This technology will be driven
hard by the fact that, even at $10 per pound, it costs a
lot of money to resupply the SPS construction base
with oxygen for 800 people. Funding will be available
to build the closed-cycle life support systems.

We'll learn how to build large manned facilities in
space suitable for large numbers of people to live in.
Parts of these habitats may have to be spun like a top
to provide a sort of pseudo-gravity from centrifugal
force; it may turn out that the physiology of human
beings demands gravity, even though people have suffered no irreversible effects from over 100 weightless
days in orbit. Of course, we will learn a great deal
about human space physiology between now and the
year 2000, too.

One of the most important things we've got to learn

about building very large habitats in space is, simply, how to keep them from leaking away an unacceptable volume of their internal atmosphere. A closed-cycle life support system may solve some of these problems, but there is only one place where lost atmospheric gas can come from: Either up out of Earth's deep and expensive gravity well or from extraterrestrial materials that are brought in and processed to release the needed gases.

We will learn, again, how people live and react in strange, isolated, dangerous environments. We already know this; we've done plenty of pioneering, and bested many frontiers on Earth. But generations often elapse between pioneering new frontiers, and old lessons must be re-learned. This time, I hope that the social sciences will have matured to the point where they can obtain some solid data from the space enterprise. It may help the social sciences pass the Swartzberg Test ("The validity of a science is its ability to predict."). We'll learn something new, too, and that will be how large groups of people will live in weightlessness where they have three dimensions in which to move.

There will come that supreme moment in the 1990s at the LEO staging base, in a Space Industrial Park in orbit, or at the GSO construction base where a man and a woman find that certain attraction between them and become the first human unit in space. After all, a human being alone is but an individual; when two human beings of opposite sex get together, they become a unit capable of reproduction. That is why it will be a supreme moment in space, and there will be no government regulations or company rules that can prevent it. Whether the first pregnant woman out there will be permitted to deliver in space remains to be seen. But the first child will be born in space before the beginning of the next century.

And, at that point, we can say that the human race has truly begun to conquer the universe because we will have taken the human family unit off the planet and into space.

But when will we have space colonies? *What do you think we've just been talking about*?

A space colony, a space settlement, a space habitat isn't just a big tin can at L5 with 100,000 people living in it. It is *any* facility in space where a single family can exist.

Every city, town, and village on Earth started with a single family, especially in the American West which is our best-remembered, if not our most recent frontier.

But will we ever see the big O'Neill colonies at L4 and L5? Certainly, but perhaps not at L4 or L5 for the military reasons discussed in the preceding chapter. But maybe *because* of those military reasons, too. However, L4 and L5 are not the only places where it would be possible to build a very large space facility in the Earth-Moon system.

Cities, whether they be on Earth or in space, are created by two factors that often exist together: Commercial and military advantage. Most European and Asian cities exist because of the combination. However, many American cities exist only because of the commercial advantage of the location and offer no defensible inner bastion against the invading hordes from over the mountains.

One of the critical aspects of early space habitats will be survivability against the radiation of solar flares. Two solutions exist: Lots of mass or the ability to get to Earth fast. Since the ability to lift heavy payloads will not be with us in the early years of the space enterprise, survival is going to be a matter of manning the life boats and getting back to the ground in a hurry. In the 1990s, the LEO base and the geosynch SPS construction base are both going to have to be equipped with "storm cellars" into which everyone can be jammed while a solar storm plays itself out. Because of weight restrictions until we can manage to obtain extraterrestrial materials and use the resulting slag as protection mass, these storm cellars are going to be anything but comfortable, spacious, or livable for long periods of time. A person will have about 36 cubic feet . . . and that's all. Not a happy prospect to relish, but who ever said that this space enterprise was going to be easy or safe?

Yes, the O'Neill habitats will come to pass, but as the result of the space enterprise; they won't create the space enterprise.

The space enterprise is the reason why people in growing numbers will be living in space during the next 50 years.

CHAPTER TWELVE

Meanwhile, back on Earth . . .

It is not possible to rationally discuss the space enterprise without taking into account what will probably happen here on Earth during the next 50 years because the space enterprise will, after all, be but a small part of the total system.

But what a part! It can be a trigger, which is a very small part of a total system whose action has far-reaching consequences beyond its apparent size and capability. It takes but a single neutron in a 32-pound sphere of 97%+ U-235 to unleash an inordinate amount of energy for a One-Second Slum Clearance Program. The space enterprise can be such a trigger on a much more benevolent explosion—the explosion of mankind toward the stars—if conditions are right. And part of our job is to make sure that those conditions occur.

The program for the space enterprise presented thus far occurs against a scenario of the future that might be termed the "baseline" scenario. More probably, it should be termed the "muddle-through" scenario. In human affairs, there has been an historic trend of very little true long-range planning and even less activity of a long-term nature. Most long-term projects in both government and business find themselves interrupted by wars, revolutions, *coup d' etats*, natural disasters, other changes in the political power structure or political control, or just plain old, everyday, run-of-the-mill expediency. The people who run the world, including politicians, bureaucrats, and business leaders, are far more concerned about the next four years than the next 40 years, about the next election of political representatives or members of the board of directors, about short-term quick–fixes to solve the problem of "my-God-how-did-we-get-into-this-mess?" This is why the baseline scenario is muddle-through and "surprise-free." It presupposes no general thermonuclear war, no major economic dislocations, no radical scientific or technological breakthroughs, no astounding natural disasters, and pretty much of a continuing evolution of today's state of affairs. The baseline scenario against which we've drawn the space enterprise thus far accepts existing forecasts of population growth, trends of change in GNP, trends of personal disposable income, trends of inflation rate (a constant average 7% per annum), forecasts of supply and demand for energy and raw materials, and general extrapolation of trends much as they have progressed historically.

However, the future is never surprise–free. The world would be a dull place indeed if we could accurately predict the future on the basis of a surprise-free scenario. As history shows, the future will be full of both little surprises and big surprises. Just look at the last decade for proof of this. But, without a baseline, muddle-through, surprise-free scenario, we have literally nothing to work with in thinking about the future. Without the baseline scenario, we cannot lay out a feasible line of progress for the space enterprise. And without a baseline scenario, we cannot make changes in that baseline and thereby create derivative scenarios. And we can't evaluate the possible effects such derivatives might have on the space enterprise.

If you don't get used to considering the future as a series of surprises, and if you don't think about what you would do if some of those took place, you'd be in a mess every time you got a flat tire; you wouldn't have the option of having an inflated spare available to bail you out of trouble on some lonely back road or even on a busy freeway. Future options are your parachute, your lifejacket, against the whims of the world.

Let's get some of the details of the baseline scenario laid out before ringing in the changes.

Present trends continue essentially unchanged. Federal and local governments continue to emphasize short-term goals less than four years into the future for political reasons. Tax laws and business regulations become more complex and restrictive, encouraging short-term views by industry. In the United States, social program costs continue to escalate at a faster rate than inflation. Politically, more and more liberal benefits are put into effect and extended to more and more people. Industrial indicators continue to show growth in spite of fluctuations, primarily due to the cleverness exhibited by entrepreneurs, managers, lawyers, and financiers working within and around the government rules and regulations. GNP, personal income, and industrial output continue to grow in the United States and other high-tech nations in response to continuing inflationary pressures caused by governments expanding their money supplies to cover deficit spending on both social programs and industrial regulation. Third World nations begin to share in this growth as they exert increased control over the export of their natural resources. Numerous international cartels come into existence, encouraged by the success of OPEC in bringing the industrialized world to its knees. No major shifts in international alignments occur, and U.S. foreign policy continues to be shaped by competition in every area with the USSR. China becomes the fulcrum of the USA/USSR competition because of the common border between China and the USSR and because China has been an historic market for domestic industry. Third World brushfire wars continue. In spite of the fact that there is continual pressure against more nations joining the nuclear arms club, one new member surfaces every three to six years.

In the baseline scenario, the space enterprise is initially fuelled by the *Star Trek* generation moving into business, industry, and government. The Space Shuttle works and Getaway Specials pay off with new discoveries. The USSR continues its space program and unveils a reusable space shuttle system of its own, sized to its unique requirements for smaller payloads. Most important, a well-known TV star and personality sees the vacuum created by the deaths or retirement of most of the old charismatic space leaders, and he moves into the vacuum to provide a cohesive center of action for the space advocates as well as the new space entrepreneurs.

Except for the continuing stimulation of trying to survive through all of the politically created crises and "shortages" by using our brains to outwit the politicians and bureaucrats (which isn't all that difficult) there really isn't anything exciting about this baseline future other than trying to keep the Neo-Luddites from bringing the world down around our ears plus the potential and human drama of the space enterprise.

Now let us take this baseline future and crank in a couple of changes. We'll create some "downside" futures plus some "upside" futures.

On the *downside:*

An energy breakthrough occurs. This could take a number of forms. OPEC could come apart under various international pressures or from within, dropping the price of petroleum. The utilities companies in the United States stage their own demonstration and simply pull the plug on all nuclear plants for 24 hours on any given day in any season of the year, followed by a shut-down of all "environmentally unacceptable" coal-fired power plants; the resulting power blackouts cause the collapse of the major environmentalist groups opposing these forms of energy. New domestic petroleum and natural gas fields are brought in. Or there is a breakthrough in the photoelectrolysis process which uses solar energy to split water into hydrogen and oxygen, which drives us very quickly into a hydrogen-based energy economy with very low costs involved. If the energy breakthrough scenario happens, it eliminates the requirement for SPS, which eliminates the need for Heavy–Lift Launch Vehicles and the other developments in space transportation that lead us to the use of extraterrestrial materials and eventually large space habitats. Left with only the communications and space materials segments of the space enterprise, things progress more slowly in space with the SPS eventually being built to supply energy for space industry in the years following 2010. The extraterrestrial materials and human habitation segments of the space enterprise are therefore set back about a quarter of a century.

An economic collapse occurs. Economists are just beginning to get a handle on some of the various economic factors that appear to behave in a cyclic fashion. For example, there is a short-term up-and-down business cycle that has a period of from three to seven years; it is an oscillation in industrial production, prices, investment levels, and employment; essentially a short-term market clearing function that balances supply and demand. There is a second, longer-term cycle of 15 to 25 years that has been tagged the Kusnets cycle; it depends on the rate of growth of capital in savings or investment and shows up as a periodic mild recession. Then there is the third cycle, a long-term 45–60 year cycle known as the Kondratieff cycle originally discovered by the Soviets and used to attempt to discredit the capitalistic system; it cycles on prices, interest rates, and investment levels. When these three cycles heterodyne and work together, as they always do, they can create very high economic peaks and very low economic valleys. These have been plotted for the boom periods of 1920 and 1960 . . . and for the economic depressions of 1830, 1890, and 1930. *If* they are real and meaningful cycles with real and meaningful keys to forecasting the future, we are entering a down-turn that we can't stop because capital is being depleted, interest rates are high, investment opportunities are limited, debt is high, and the financial system is overextended. The capital demands for the energy industry alone in the next few decades, exclusive of the SPS system, appear to be staggeringly large. The traditional share of net private capital investment has been 25% to 30%, but the requirements for the energy industry alone could push this up to 65% by the late 1980s. A flow of money is like the flow of blood in an individual; if it slows or stops, there is trouble. If we do indeed face an economic collapse as a future scenario, we can expect that the space enterprise will be delayed by at least 25 years.

A disenchantment with space occurs. To quote Gerald W. Driggers who was the team leader of the recent space industrialization study carried out by Science Applications, Inc. for NASA, "It appears that private industry cannot step up to the total challenge. If the public sector does not, then we are probably witnessing one of the key non-actions leading to the general demise of the United States as a future leader. Unless space begins in less than ten years to generate a highly visible return on investment, we can expect an even greater public disinterest than previously experienced. At that point the Shuttle will be considered a fraud and the whole concept of space industrialization just another way to flim-flam the politicians into wasting money to keep overpaid bureaucrats on the payroll." The Space Shuttle could be dragged out in time by a reduction of federal funding in favor of spending on a series of new "Quality of Life" programs proclaimed by the President and Congress as the theme of the 1980s. Or the Space Shuttle could continue to experience massive cost overruns due to the advanced nature of its technology. Or the Space Shuttle could suffer an ignoble failure caused by some simple technician's mistake which kills the crew and destroys the entire vehicle. Or because of the increasing pressures of inflation, the political energy crisis, or a perceived continuing decline in the quality of life (real or not), people lose interest in space because they are simply trying to maintain what they can of a pre-existing lifestyle. Or they are trying to survive. All of these things can bring the space enterprise to a halt in the United States. But it will probably not bring it to a complete worldwide halt. The USSR will continue its program, and the results from that Soviet program will goad Japan and Europe into the space enterprise on their own . . . 20 years from now.

So much for the "downside" scenarios, and these

three are just a sample; there are more. Work up your own and not only learn how futurists do it, but also learn how to prepare for the future yourself.

Let's look at three possible "upside" scenarios.

A challenge of foreign space advances is a scenario that has already been played in the first act of the space race. The Soviet *Sputnik-I* flung a challenge at America; most people believe it was a space race challenge, but as one of the few people who brought to public attention that *Sputnik-I* was a national security challenge because it was launched with an ICBM, I can personally guarantee that it was *not* viewed by the government as a prestige challenge. The U.S.A. won that contest when the Soviets opted out of the Moon race in December 1968 by saying that they had never been racing in the first place (like hell they weren't!). Some people may think that a foreign space challenge scenario is unrealistic, that having once played the game that we will not do it again. Consider some of the triggers that might set off real international competition in the space enterprise. First, France demonstrates the capability to place one ton in GSO with *Ariane* at a cost less than the U.S. can do it with the Space Shuttle. Suppose the current situation in the communications satellite industry worsens and that foreign companies not only manage to outbid American firms for such space hardware as momentum control wheels, but for whole satellites; if foreign electronics and aerospace firms capture all or a majority of the contracts for construction of *Intelsats*, weather satellites, and Earth resources satellites, this becomes a major economic and business challenge, not the political challenge that the Moon race was. The Japanese already have the capability to place large payloads in geosynchronous orbit; when and if they purchase a

Space Shuttle, they suddenly provide competition to the USA. The Japanese certainly have the ability to acquire the technology to build their own Shuttle, as they have amply proven with other aerospace items, and strong competition could arise there because the Japanese will certainly strive to make their shuttle more economical. Consider the fact that the Europeans may suddenly decide to do their own shuttle by purchasing the system from U.S. companies, by purchasing a Japanese vehicle, or by an arrangement with the Soviets to buy or use the smaller USSR shuttle. Another trigger to this scenario could come from one or more European space processing breakthroughs made by their scientists riding in their *SpaceLab* aboard the NASA Space Shuttle whose development was paid for by U.S. tax dollars; this will cause a great stir on Capitol Hill and an uproar in the American industrial heartland. The ultimate challenge could come again from the USSR in any combination of events; the Soviets develop important new alloys in space or they are able to process better electronic semiconductor materials in space. The Soviets may get their very large *Saturn-V* type launch vehicle working (although it appears to have been put on the back burner at this time), and this gives them a Heavy–Lift Launch Vehicle capability that we cannot match; with their big vehicles, they begin to assemble their own space collective factory in orbit, their version of the proposed Space Industrial Park. With a reusable shuttle, a large launch vehicle, and a LEO base, the Soviets are then well on their way to building their version of the SPS, which is a project of the size, scope, and grandeur they seem particularly attracted to in view of their massive hydroelectric projects in the past decades. In this scenario, economic competition is the driver, and it could result in a number of reactions on the part of the United States and its industry. First of all, there would be a push from within domestic industry to meet the competition. Secondly, there would be a reaction with the federal government which would result in measures being adopted to assist American industry to meet the competition. There are numerous sub–scenarios to this one. But, as I think you'll agree now, it is not the "play-it-again-Sam" scenario of the Moon race all over again.

A commitment to space is made by the President of the United States with the backing of Congress. The present void in the national political scene of any strong supporter of a space effort, particularly in the Executive Branch, presents an opportunity for political exploitation by any politician who grasps the meaning and potential of the space enterprise. There are at present several Senators and members of Congress who are aware of the space enterprise, and they are a strong nucleus in Congress that is now at considerable odds with the administration. I have sat in congressional hearing rooms and heard members of Congress square-off against administration science and space leaders who were publicly accused of being short-sighted, conservative, foot-dragging bureaucrats . . . and who actually projected a public image consistent with that congressional charge! In view of the plethora of space-related resolutions, acts, and new legislation that have come before Congress since 1976, it would not be surprising to see a government commitment to the space enterprise for both political and economic purposes. A massive government commitment to the space enterprise could take the form of increased NASA funding to develop the Heavy–Lift Launch Vehicle, the follow–on to the Shuttle, the manned orbital transfer vehicle, and various other pieces of space hardware. The government could offer strong incentives for industrial participation in the space enterprise in the form of government-guaranteed loads. A strong inducement to industrial participation in the space enterprise could come if the government sets up a "heads, we all win; tails, nobody loses" situation—for example, allowing a company to pay no taxes whatsoever on profits made from the space enterprise for a period of years. What is the rationale behind such a scenario? The politicians can use it for political gain because it will create new jobs, increase the GNP, lower unemployment, encourage new technology to meet foreign competition, and increase the net tax base. This is particularly true of any government commitment to an SPS program to relieve energy demand. There are ample political reasons for supporting highly visible high technology that becomes publicly available and publicly useful in a reasonably short period of time—which was *not* the case with the manned lunar landing program which had no apparent immediate public utility. The space enterprise does, and this "commitment to space" scenario is a highly probable "upside" variation of the baseline scenario.

Finally, the *space entrepreneurs* have initial successes in the space processing field, are able to overcome bureaucratic and legal obstacles to commercial ventures in space, and manage to obtain enough venture capital to reach the turnover point that insures enough capital resources to eliminate the current business dogma of the space enterprise being "too risky." It would take success by only a few companies early in the 1980 decade to stimulate further innovation and competition, not only by domestic firms but by foreign and multinational corporations. International Satellite Industries, Inc., the first staging corporation, raises the capital it needs (some of it from Mid-Eastern sources) and runs through its programmed sequence of investment followed by operation. Others follow. The initial experiments vital to the SPS system decision are so positive in nature that the domestic electrical power industry makes a long-term commitment to the SPS system, utilizing capital funds previously earmarked for construction of either nuclear or coal power plants. Boeing is successful in its effort to acquire the Space Shuttle from the government and begins to operate it as a commercial venture. The West German firm of OTRAG, formed to develop a privately funded space launch vehicle system capable of low-cost operation, overcomes political problems by allying with several equatorial governments of the Third World who are successful in blocking Soviet and western world opposition in the UN. A space freeport such as envisioned by the Sabre Foundation becomes a reality in one or more equatorial nations, giving the Third World a piece of the action in the space enterprise. Rockwell International makes good on its announced plan to be the first commercial company to make a profit from a product made in space. Any of these triggers can result in a change to the baseline scenario that turns it into an upside private enterprise scenario.

There are some interesting consequences that become apparent from a study of the baseline scenario, the three downside scenarios, and the three upside scenarios. First of all, the downside scenarios do not *prevent* the space enterprise from taking place; they merely *delay* it by 25 years at the most. This is not too late to have the space enterprise make a significant contribution to heading off the long-term reality of a limits-to-growth future. However, if the downside scenarios become real futures that delay the space enterprise beyond 2025, our grandchildren are in very serious trouble.

The upside scenarios considered, plus several that have not been discussed here because of their lower probability, do not significantly advance the time schedule of the space enterprise as laid out in the baseline scenario. Just because a woman can have a baby in nine months does not mean that it is possible to have the baby in one month by putting nine women on the job. The development of new technology occurs in spurts of innovation followed by long periods of gestation and conservative development. Engineers are basically highly conservative people, preferring to introduce only one new element at a time into a well-understood system and then carefully checking the effects of the new element. Without this basic conservatism, nuclear reactors might indeed melt down instead of going into fail-safe shut-down, more wings and engines might fall off airplanes, and automobile manufacturers would be put completely out of business by recalls. The upside scenarios only *insure* that the space enterprise is going to move along more or less as forecast in the baseline scenario. They turn a 50–50 proposition of the baseline scenario into a show–stopping sure bet. At most the baseline space enterprise time table is advanced perhaps five years in some areas.

There are other scenarios that could be considered. Some of them have a very low probability of occurring (which does not mean that they will not occur, but that they are less likely to occur than the six variations we've talked about). Or they are bizarre, depending upon serendipitous breakthroughs of a highly unusual nature. For example, I think we can eliminate the possibility of contact by extraterrestrial intelligence; it is possible, but it is such a wild card that we cannot do anything except acknowledge that it might happen and be flexible enough to work with it if it does. We can also rule out a scenario that uses a shortage of critical materials to drive the space enterprise, particularly in the area of extraterrestrial materials; there is no real, physical shortage in the cards out to the year 2025 except as artificially created by people for political/economic reasons. A future in which a major ecological disaster occurs is also a long shot: Despite a great deal of attention to air pollution, water pollution, and despoilment of the land and sea by mining, industrial, and municipal wastes, there appear to be no sources of pollution, including nuclear, that are capable of producing a nationwide, let alone a global, impact of major epidemic or economic significance. There are several technical long shots that could create a viable scenario but involve unknown factors; among these are the development of a space drive other than the rocket and the creation of artificial intelligence, the man-computer link-up, and the intelligence amplifier. The one technical long shot for the future that may be the real sleeper results from progress in the biological sciences and attendant advances in biotechnology. If, for example, life expectancy could be increased to 150–180 years (as many researchers now believe it can), this can have a profound impact upon the space enterprise that results, surprisingly, in a downside scenario.

There is one scenario that was not presented here. This one considers a future without the space enterprise. At this time, it can be considered to be the most unlikely of all mainly because the space enterprise is already under way. A complete failure of will, nerve, or imagination on the part of Americans will not stop it because the Soviets are already up there engaged in it. The vacuum created by an American failure in the space enterprise will simply draw in Japan and Europe to a greater degree than they have already committed.

The only scenario in which the space enterprise does not happen is the one where it is *prevented* from happening by a general, all-out thermonuclear war with multi-megaton warhead exchanges. Everyone immediately thinks of the United States vs. the Soviet Union; but there is a much higher probability that it could occur between the Soviet Union and the People's Republic of China. The outcome may be a return to barbarism by the world. But one must recall the classic remark made by the space pioneer Willy Ley: "There will always be survivors!"

There *will* be survivors with a high technology at their command if the space enterprise grows and progresses. Once the communications, industrial, energy, and materials base of our planet is transferred—even if only in part—to the Solar System, it can form a foundation for rebuilding the Earth following any major military political mistake that results in general war. To paraphrase Sir Winston Churchill, the space enterprise with its power and technology intact could step forth to the rescue and liberation of the world.

It is an option that we should not overlook.

And it is another reason why the space enterprise *must* and *will* take place.

EPILOGUE

The space enterprise has already started. It now involves more than a billion dollars per year. It is growing. Approximately 10% of what we have talked about is history; the remaining 90% remains to be done in the next 50 years or less. As we have probed deeper into the future of the space enterprise, our crystal ball has become more cloudy. Yet it has revealed some very exciting things.

First of all, the space enterprise appears to offer something for everybody because, at its roots, it contains the promise of helping us improve our lives and living conditions as well as those of our children. It offers some solutions to our national and world problems, both short-term and long-term. It offers a chance for all to participate and benefit. It offers the real hope of eliminating ecological damage to the Earth's biosphere from industrial and energy-producing activities.

If I have seemed a bit harsh on the environmentalists herein, it is not because I believe in further despoilage of planet Earth, but only that we cannot eliminate the dangers to our planetary home by regressing into the past and failing to use our brains to solve our problems. The only way out of our problems is *through* them, not wallowing in them. If we do things right, if we plan things carefully, and if we are clever, bright, intelligent, creative, and compassionate, we can bring to pass a garden planet of plenty supported by an industrial base located elsewhere in a more benevolent industrial environment. *Everybody wins.*

But the space enterprise doesn't suffer from some of the shortcomings of past space ventures. It is more than exploring the universe to ferret out its secrets. It is more than some high philosophical goal involving esoteric considerations of the ultimate destiny of the human race. It is a pragmatic, realistic, practical, sound, and economical activity that answers the question, "What's in it for me?" The answer: "Everything." For everyone everywhere on Earth.

The space enterprise is an economic activity and has value of various kinds . . . lots of value. Consider the United States alone:

By the year 2010, according to some very conservative forecasts and estimates, the space enterprise will create at least 1,900,000 new jobs that are directly related to the activity out of a projected work force of more than 250,000,000 people. It will generate each year salaries and wages of more than $4 billion. It will expand the tax base by $20 billion. Its annual contribution to the Gross National Product of 2010 can be as large as $800 billion or about 10% of the GNP projected for that time. Because the industries, products, and services of the space enterprise are exportable, they can improve American balance of trade figures by as much as $50 billion per year by 2010.

Beyond the figures, the space enterprise gives Americans something they dearly love: A frontier to enrich our national pride and aspirations. It is something to do, and we know how to do it because we have done things like it before.

The space enterprise will affect not only Americans, but it will raise the worldwide standard of living. It provides improved communications that lead to better understanding and better educational opportunities. It will provide better products to do jobs better, and it will do this without further depleting the Earth of irreplaceable raw materials. It will provide solar energy in abundance to places that today still depend upon the ancient energy sources of human and animal muscle power.

Space scientists who are today battling to prevent the use of the Space Shuttle for the space enterprise so that they can make use of its limited planned missions will suddenly find themselves capable of doing much more space science riding on the coattails of the space enterprise. The only way to get enough space transportation to permit more space science to be done is to support the growth of the space enterprise which will require this space transportation. Science and industry support one another; industry knows this, and it is time that science wakes up to the fact, too.

The shadow of high cost is still cast upon the space enterprise, but it is unwarranted. If we do everything that we have forecast to be possible in the baseline scenario, the total investment in the space enterprise by 2010 will be about $200 billion with a maximum annual capital requirement of $15 billion per year. A lot of money? Here is some perspective: In 1977, $340.5 billion was raised in the United States by means of both long-term and short-term notes and bonds. Domestic industry spent $132 billion in capital investment on plant and equipment. In the same year of 1977, the utility industry spent $26.1 billion on new plants and equipment for the generation and distribution of electricity. One public utility alone is raising $4 billion at the rate of $600 million to $800 million per year for the construction of two new power plants.

When we eliminate the high risk of the space enterprise that currently is a stumbling block to the needed investment of capital, the capital is there.

We know that the revenue potentials are there when we can prove that the data is hard. The Space Shuttle must fly. The *SpaceLab* must be used. The groundwork in space products and space energy must be carried out . . . and soon.

The sooner we do it, the sooner we can reap the benefits.

The times are right.

If we wait, they may not be.

Serious international competition already exists and is building rapidly.

Others elsewhere already know what you now know. Nobody has bothered to tell you about it before; few believed that it was real. Or could be real.

Once the risk is lowered, the space enterprise can be realized with tools that private enterprise already works with. Public and private investment in the space enterprise in the 1980 decade will be paid back manyfold in the 1990s and beyond.

By invoking the proven factor of self-interest, the space enterprise is the catalyst that is needed to boost all of us upward toward the next plateau of human achievement—an achievement *en toto*, not just in space or on planet Earth, but throughout the multitude of activities that is the human endeavor.

What happens if we, as Americans, do not take the leadership role in the space enterprise? What happens if we do not do any or all of these things?

The space enterprise will still be there. Others will then have the exclusive opportunity to exploit it. And they will do so. If Americans dislike what OPEC is doing with petroleum now, it is just the beginning; others will do the same with other raw materials and with the products and services from a non-American space enterprise. If others build an SPS system, we will pay their prices for the energy of the Sun. We will follow the path of the great nations and peoples of the past who missed great opportunities and opted to let others take the risks instead . . . and thereby set themselves on the long, rocky, disastrous road downward. This could easily happen, given the tenor of the times in America; intellectuals, the news media, and uninformed people are beginning to question the ability of technology to solve our problems. They are right: Technology alone cannot, but people using technology can. In fact, it's the only way the problems can be solved. Would mystic chanting work better? It hasn't in the past. And the problems will not go away if we exhibit the Ostrich Syndrome.

The next decade is critical for us. This opportunity must not be missed.

"There is a tide in the affairs of men,
  Which, taken at the flood, leads on to fortune;
  Omitted, all the voyage of their life
  Is bound in shallows and in miseries.
  On such a full sea are we now afloat,
  And we must take the current when it serves,
  Or lose our venture . . ."

That is the way William Shakespeare put it in *Julius Ceasar* (Act IV, Scene 3).

But we don't need to look to the great thinkers of the past to find support for the space enterprise. Some of the best minds of our own era have seen or sensed what we have spoken of herein and expressed their own thoughts.

Norman Cousins: "On the one hand are those who see a human being as a product of happenstance: they have no difficulty in separating people from their prospects. They attach sovereignty to the glory of numbers and cost-benefit ratios rather than to unlimited human development. On the other hand are those who define a human being as a species whose uniqueness is represented by the ability to do something for the first time, a species capable of comprehending the cause of its agonies—capable, too, of transforming great expectations into realities. Those who take this enlarged view of the nature of the human being will not close the door on the greatest frontier of all, a frontier in which the infinities of the human mind and outer space will become congruent and indeed perfectly matched."

Alfred North Whitehead: "There is no choice before us. Either we must succeed in providing the rational coordination of impulses and guts, or for centuries civilization will sink into a mere welter of minor excitements. We must produce a great age or see the collapse of the upward striving of the race."

James A. Michener: "My own life has been spent chronicling the rise and fall of human systems, and I am convinced that we are all terribly vulnerable . . . We should be reluctant to turn back upon the frontier of this epoch. Space is indifferent to what we do; it has no feeling, no design, no interest in whether we grapple with it or not. But we cannot be indifferent to space, because the grand slow march of intelligence

The year: 2019. The place: The "Kitty Hawk" of the Moon. Three touristing has disturbed even the flag at Tranquility Base.

has brought us, in our generation, to a point from which we can explore and understand and utilize it. To turn back now would be to deny our history, our capabilities."

The Honorable Dr. Harrison H. Schmitt, the United States Senator from New Mexico: "What does it take for Americans to do great things; to go to the Moon, to win wars, to dig canals between oceans, to build a railroad across a continent? In independent thought about this question, Neil Armstrong and I concluded that it takes a coincidence of four conditions, or, in Neil's view, the simultaneous peaking of four of the many cycles of American life. First, a base of technology must exist from which the thing to be done can be

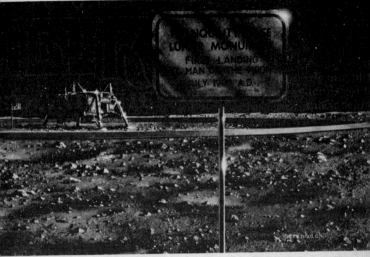

have the inevitable photograph snapped by their guide. After 50 years, noth-

done. Second, a period of national uneasiness about America's place in the scheme of human activities must exist. Third, some catalytic event must occur that focuses the national attention on the direction to proceed. Finally, an articulate and wise leader must sense these first three conditions and put forth with words and action the great thing to be accomplished. The motivation of young Americans to do what needs to be done flows from such a coincidence of conditions . . . The Tom Jeffersons, the Teddy Roosevelts, and the John Kennedys will appear. We must begin to create the tools of leadership which they, and their young frontiersmen, will require to lead us onward and upward."

America is the only frontier-bred culture of modern times with the social organizations, the capital resources, the technology, and the industrial base to carry forward the space enterprise. We lack only the national will to do it.

As Americans, we and our forefathers did not create this, a nation with an economy and culture totally unique and unmatched in all human history, by sitting timidly on the Atlantic Coast of this continent, facing an untamed wilderness that began a hundred miles from our modest seaport cities. We did not simply talk about the problems and study them; we got out there, rolled up our sleeves, took huge risks, worked hard, turned a wilderness into the wonder of the world, and often died in the process. Many people said that the wilderness was useless; we discovered otherwise and made it useful.

We now face another frontier, not a hundred miles inland, but a hundred miles over our heads. Twenty years ago, it seemed as hostile and alien as the Great Wilderness must have seemed to our forefathers. But we have explored this new frontier and we have discovered that we can use it. Following what our forefathers have taught us, we can turn it into something of great value that will bring benefits to the people of America and the world.

The space enterprise is not going to be easy.

The space enterprise is not going to come cheap.

But the space enterprise will have a payoff that will far exceed our wildest dreams.

We only have to do it.

We *can* do it.

We *will* do it.

We *must* do it!

APPENDIX
FOR MORE INFORMATION

(Author's note: There is now far too much information available on the space enterprise for me to list a bibliography. The following organizations and government sources are your best bet for keeping up with or getting more information about specific areas of the space enterprise that are of interest to you.)

American Astronautical Society, 6060 Duke Street, Alexandria, VA 22304.

American Institute of Aeronautics and Astronautics, 1290 Avenue of the Americas, New York, NY 10019

Committee for the Future, 2325 Porter Street N.W., Washington, DC 20008.

Federation for the Advancement of Students in Science and Technology (FASST), 1785 Massachusetts Avenue, N.W., Washington, DC 20036.

L-5 Society, 1620 North Park Ave., Tucson, AZ 85719.

Lunar and Planetary Institute, 3303 NASA Road One, Houston, TX 77058.

National Action Committee for Space, P.O. Box 5001, Washington, DC 20004.

National Association of Rocketry, P.O. Box 725, New Providence, NJ 07974.

National Space Institute, 1911 N. Fort Myer Drive, Suite 408, Arlington, VA 22209.

Sabre Foundation, 221 West Carillo Street, Santa Barbara, CA 93101.

Space Studies Institute, P.O. Box 82, Princeton, NJ 08540.

Sunsat Energy Council, 600 New Hampshire Avenue, Suite 480, Washington, DC 20031.

Universities Space Research Association, P.O. Box 903, Columbia, MD 21044.

National Aeronautics and Space Administration, Public Affairs Office, Washington, DC 20546.

George C. Marshall Space Flight Center, Code LA41, NASA, Marshall Space Flight Center, AL 35812.

NASA Ames Research Center, Mountain View, CA 94035.

NASA Goddard Space Flight Center, Greenbelt, MD 20771.

NASA Jet Propulsion Laboratory, 4800 Oak Grove Drive, Pasadena, CA 91103.

NASA Johnson Space Center, Houston, TX 77058.

Assistant Secretary for Energy Research, Satellite Power Systems Office, U.S. Department of Energy, Washington, DC 20545.

FRED SABERHAGEN

MORE TRADE SCIENCE FICTION

Ace Books is proud to publish these latest works by major SF authors in deluxe large format collectors' editions. Many are illustrated by top artists such as Alicia Austin, Esteban Maroto and Fernando.

Robert A. Heinlein	Expanded Universe	21883	$8.95
Frederik Pohl	Science Fiction: Studies in Film (illustrated)	75437	$6.95
Frank Herbert	Direct Descent (illustrated)	14897	$6.95
Harry G. Stine	The Space Enterprise (illustrated)	77742	$6.95
Ursula K. LeGuin and Virginia Kidd	Interfaces	37092	$5.95
Marion Zimmer Bradley	Survey Ship (illustrated)	79110	$6.95
Hal Clement	The Nitrogen Fix	58116	$6.95
Andre Norton	Voorloper	86609	$6.95
Orson Scott Card	Dragons of Light (illustrated)	16660	$7.95

Available wherever paperbacks are sold or use this coupon.

Gordon R. Dickson

☐	16015	Dorsai!	1.95
☐	34256	Home From The Shore	2.25
☐	56010	Naked To The Stars	1.95
☐	63160	On The Run	1.95
☐	68023	Pro	1.95
☐	77417	Soldier, Ask Not	1.95
☐	77765	The Space Swimmers	1.95
☐	77749	Spacial Deliver	1.95
☐	77803	The Spirit Of Dorsai	2.50

Available wherever paperbacks are sold or use this coupon.

ACE SCIENCE FICTION
P.O. Box 400, Kirkwood, N.Y. 13795

Please send me the titles checked above. I enclose _____.
Include 75¢ for postage and handling if one book is ordered; 50¢ per
book for two to five. If six or more are ordered, postage is free. California, Illinois, New York and Tennessee residents please add sales tax.

NAME_____

ADDRESS_____

CITY_____STATE_____ZIP_____

148

FAFHRD AND THE
GRAY MOUSER
SAGA

☐ 79176	SWORDS AND DEVILTRY	$2.25
☐ 79156	SWORDS AGAINST DEATH	$2.25
☐ 79185	SWORDS IN THE MIST	$2.25
☐ 79165	SWORDS AGAINST WIZARDRY	$2.25
☐ 79223	THE SWORDS OF LANKHMAR	$1.95
☐ 79169	SWORDS AND ICE MAGIC	$2.25

Current and Recent
Ace Science Fiction Releases
of Special Interest, As Selected
by the Editor of <u>Destinies</u>

Ursula K. Le Guin